Born Under The Clouds

Born Under The Clouds

B A Jones

First edition 2022

Book design by Publishing Push

ISBN 978-1-80227-312-0 (paperback)
ISBN 978-1-80227-724-1 (ebook)

Typeset using Atomik ePublisher from Easypress Technologies

PART I

Chapter 1

A Baby Girl Was Born

It was 5 pm on a very wet and cold winter's night, November 13th, 1953. The weather was horrendous; the clashing of the clouds, the sound of the thunder, and the lighting up of the sky. It was then that Gladys went into labour with her second child. The midwife was called to assist in the home birth of Mrs Gladys Thomas who resided at 13 Mountain Crescent. Teresa, the midwife, arrived soaking wet as she had cycled to the address, and still safely delivered a baby girl weighing in at 8lb 5oz. Due to her braving the weather and because of her kindness and support during the birth, and not having decided on a name for her baby girl, Gladys asked the midwife her name. The midwife said, "It's Teresa, and I would be honoured to give her my name." Gladys answered, "Thank you; that's now her name!"

So it was that Teresa Thomas was born into the world with her identity all intact. The midwife left the house happily; not only had she safely delivered a baby girl but she also had her name, and thankfully, the storm had passed ensuring a dry ride back to base. Meanwhile, in the bedroom, mother Gladys was holding baby Teresa, with proud father Michael looking on. They were both so pleased as they also had a son called Terry and now had both a girl and a boy. Terry was one and a half years old, and he was called into the bedroom to meet his baby sister. Terry didn't like his sister very much and ran out of the bedroom screaming. "I don't like it," he said, but not really fazed by his reaction, Gladys and Michael carried on as normal in the hope that he would come around to the idea, and eventually, and slowly, a bond between the siblings began to grow.

Times were different now since the war had finished eight years before. Lots of changes were taking place in the country, and, by this time, rationing had come to an end. Sugar was readily available, but some meat was still hard to come by. This was the year that the new 'buy now, pay later' ethos emerged, and workers were joining the unions in their thousands.

Times were hard financially for Gladys and Michael, although he had a good office job in the steelworks, and Gladys stayed at home like most married women, looking after the children and keeping house. Usually, it was only the men who would go out to work in order to support the family. They lived in a semi-detached three-bedroom council house, which sat on a hill on the main bus route at the bottom of the council estate, and the rent was paid weekly. Gladys was originally from London and had come to Wales as a refugee in June 1941 during the war. The Germans were bombing London and the children were evacuated by train and bus to Wales, which was thought to be a designated reception area, as were all industrial valleys in Wales. Gladys never really settled; she always wanted to return to London but thought she was very lucky not to be placed with a Welsh-speaking family, as that would have been very stressful. Her adopted parents were kind and fair, and she gained a brother called Connor.

Michael, however, lived in a much better house with his mother Jane, who was a live-in housekeeper for Uncle Ben. Ben owned his semi-detached house; it was away from the council estates in a nice middle-class area. At the age of eighteen, Michael joined the Royal Navy and worked on the submarines during the war. However, when the war ended on the 2nd of September 1945, he found returning to civilian life was a real struggle for him. Eventually, after careful thought, Michael decided to be a male nurse. Now, this was an excellent idea, until the exams. Michael suffered badly with his nerves and, although he knew the answers, the stress got the better of him and he walked out of the exam room! Several attempts were made, but each time he tried, his nerves would set in. Because of this, Michael decided to work for a steel company in which he progressed to a well-paid office job.

As they grew, Terry and Teresa, or the two Ts as they were called by their parents, were starting to notice their surroundings and the atmosphere they were living in. Teresa would wake up crying and scared due to noises downstairs. Her brother would be looking down from the landing, having also been woken. The siblings were too young to understand, but every time they woke up, they would be resettled back to sleep by Gladys. This became a normal thing for the siblings to witness, but their fear grew stronger as they started to grow up and the rows just carried on.

Teresa was three years old when another baby girl was born to Gladys and Michael. Her name was Tabitha, so that made three Ts in the family. Teresa remembers her Nana Jane coming over to see the new baby. Teresa never liked her Nana Jane because she used to pull her cheeks and it hurt her. She would also bring fruit but not for the children, just for her daddy, Michael, as he was her son. Gladys never liked Nana Jane because she always said that Gladys wasn't good enough for her son. It had also been said that they had a massive fight while Gladys was pregnant with Terry, and literally, knives were being pulled in the kitchen. Gladys apparently said, "Let the best bugger win". At the time, they were all living together while Michael and Gladys were waiting for a council house but they never got on. Teresa liked her other nana and grandpa who lived down the road. Her grandpa would knit scarves on a piece of wood with nails in the top, and her nana would always have sweets in a tin on the fireplace; they used to call them market sweets as they bought them from the marketplace. Their house always smelt musky, and heavy, a smell you don't forget. Uncle Connor lived there, Gladys's adopted brother; he was a very quiet man and he had a girlfriend called May. They were planning their wedding which wasn't very far away.

As Teresa grew, she became more aware of her outside surroundings and children playing in the street - the neighbours' children, who were extremely naughty and had dirty faces - one of them even ate a worm (yuck). The women would wear headscarves covering their hair, and long pinafores over their clothes, and they would talk at the gates and over their fences whilst smoking cigarettes. Pretty ladies would walk by in their high heels and men would wolf-whistle as they passed. Neighbours would live in each other's houses and borrow things like a bowl of sugar. Facts showed that anyone born on a council estate would grow up faster and become very streetwise, because they weren't wrapped in cotton wool and very much had to fend for themselves in a lot of ways.

Teresa's father Michael would plant their back garden with vegetables and put flowers in the borders, a pastime he really enjoyed. One day, whilst he was digging in the garden, the neighbour next door asked Michael if Teresa was allowed a kitten. Knowing how much she liked animals, Michael said,

"Yes". Teresa was beaming! She called her kitten Fluffy and she became very close to her cat. She would put Fluffy in her doll's pram and the neighbours would tell her mother, "Your Teresa has a dead cat in her pram!" Gladys would say, "No, Fluffy is very much alive and does stay there if Teresa puts her there". They were completely inseparable. Teresa loved Fluffy; she even slept on her bed. Teresa always found comfort and joy with her furry best and only friend. She was very much attached, a feeling she truly found new.

Chapter 2

Tensions Progress as Teresa Starts School

As she was now five years old, it was time for Teresa to start school but because the new intake's cut-off point was the first of September, she had to wait for the Easter intake to start school. Therefore, Teresa was several months older than other new intakes at the infant school when she started. On the very first day of school, Teresa was swinging on the front gate of her house while waiting for her mother to take her to school. She had her new clothes on, and brand-new black patent shoes. She was singing away happily when suddenly, the loud angry voice of her mother shouted, "Get off the gate! God help you if you scratch those new shoes". Teresa did what she was told and got off the gate. She had the feeling her mother was not happy as she angrily put Tabitha into her pushchair, grabbed Terry and Teresa and made her way up the hill to the school.

Teresa enjoyed school; she made new friends and could paint and colour, but she hated school dinners. She asked her mother if she could come home for dinner. She went on to say, "I don't like them; they make me eat salad cream and I don't like it". Her request was refused with Gladys saying, "I have enough to do with you three kids without picking you up and taking you back." The atmosphere at home was scary, so the children went out to play whenever they could, drawing hopscotch with coloured chalk on the pavement outside the house, and other children from houses nearby would join them. The pavements were well-trodden with people going up and down, and some got angry, telling the children off as they blocked their way.

However, winter soon came, meaning they were not allowed out to play as it was too cold. Gladys bought Teresa a new hat and coat, which came complete with a hand muff to keep her hands warm; Terry had a smart coat with a brown suede collar but he hated it. One day, whilst at her bedroom window, Teresa heard the sound of a man shouting, "Rag and bone, rag and bone, sixpence or a goldfish!" She had never heard this before. She saw people taking things to him and he would give them sixpence or a goldfish. Teresa ran to her mum and pleaded, "Can I have a goldfish?" Gladys replied, "No, you cannot; you have a cat, and the cat will eat your goldfish." Teresa ran off crying, saying, "You're mean, you are; you're mean! Fluffy wouldn't eat a goldfish".

Terry had a mouse that he kept in a cage in the shed out the back. When he went into the shed one day, he found he had lots of mice as his mouse was a girl and she had given birth. Terry ran into the house and asked his mum if he could bring the mice indoors, as it was warmer for the baby mice, but Gladys replied, "No! I don't like mice and you will have to get rid of them". Terry burst into tears and told Gladys to fuck off. Gladys was peeling potatoes in the sink, and with that, she turned around and slapped Terry in the face, hitting him hard enough to push him into the hallway. Teresa hadn't seen behaviour like this before so she ran into the bedroom, followed by a very upset Terry. Teresa and Terry heard arguments downstairs all the time but had never witnessed angry violence like that before. Teresa couldn't even understand why Terry got slapped as she had never heard those words before. Both sat in the bedroom consoling each other and looking at the marks on Terry's face made by Gladys's wet hands as she hadn't stopped to dry them before hitting Terry. Both siblings stayed out of Gladys's way in shock. Michael came home from work and Terry and Teresa listened on the stairs whilst Gladys was telling him what had happened. They heard Michael say, "Well, where did he get that from?" Gladys replied, "Bloody school, that's where". Minutes later, she called upstairs to Terry and Teresa; "Dinner's ready!" It was egg and chips. They all sat down at the table then Teresa said, "We had chips yesterday," to which Gladys replied, "No, you didn't, you had fritters." Teresa thought they were the same thing but a different shape, which they were, of course. A sack of potatoes was always there in the pantry, and Gladys had a new kitchen tool which made the chips crinkle cut, so now there were three different-shaped meals on the teatime table.

Weeks went by before Teresa heard the rag and bone man again in the street. Gladys was hanging the washing out, so Teresa hurried downstairs, grabbed her new coat and muff, and took it to the rag and bone man. He said to the little girl, "Does your mother know what you're doing?" Teresa replied, "Yes, it's too small for me". With that, Teresa got her goldfish and hurried back to her house carrying the goldfish in a plastic bag. Gladys spotted her and went mad! She stopped what she was doing, took the goldfish from Teresa and hurried up the street to get her coat back. Teresa hid behind the kitchen table, and when Gladys came in, she smacked Teresa very hard on the legs and sent her to bed. Terry found this very funny and told Teresa, "Hahaha, you got slapped now!" The siblings started fighting, hitting as hard as they could, when Gladys came in and dragged Terry out, slapped him as well and he too was sent to bed. That evening, neither Terry nor Teresa was allowed back downstairs, so Michael took a jam sandwich up for both siblings.

Terry and Teresa were growing up fast, but Tabitha was the baby of the house; she could do anything. She never got slapped, even when she pushed her tin pram with her dolly in it straight through Terry's and Teresa's building-block towers. They both told Gladys she was spoiling their game, but they were told, "She's only a baby; she's the youngest". So, they felt she could do no wrong as not once did Tabitha get told off or slapped.

The siblings were noticing a lot more as they grew up, like when to run and when to shut up. The time came for Terry to begin junior school as he was now seven and Teresa wouldn't be long in following him as there were only eighteen months between them. Terry felt very much the big boy now and he was growing up rapidly, playing football with older kids on the estate. He was also picking up bad habits and was told by Michael and Gladys who he could play with and who he couldn't play with. The loud arguments were continuing as usual downstairs, with Gladys shouting to Michael, "Oh yes, your mother's always right; you've been to see her again. I will go and give her a piece of my mind". With that, furniture was being thrown, the coffee table hit the window as it smashed into pieces, ornaments were being smashed, and Gladys was shouting, "No, Michael, no!" On the landing, Terry and Teresa were watching through the banister rails, too frightened to move, and knew Michael was beating up Gladys. He shouted, "Yes, my mother is right about you." Tabitha was crying inconsolably at the bedroom door; this fight had woken her for the first time. It was much more violent this time, with Gladys sporting a black eye and sore ribs.

After that night, all was quiet in the house for a few days, but then one day, during the weekend, Gladys took Teresa's hand and said, "You're coming with me today." Terry and Tabitha stayed with the neighbour next door while Gladys held Teresa's hand and took her down the hill from the house and over the bridge. They were never usually allowed to go over this bridge; only uphill for school. The steps on the bridge were worn in the middle. You would go up about twelve steps, then flat across over the railway line, then down another lot of steps which turned to the right on the last two. Teresa was holding her mother's hand and remembered going past a bus station and a place that said 'free house'. "Can we go and live there, Mum, because it's free?" Gladys laughed and explained it was a pub and they were allowed to sell whatever beer they liked; it was not a house. They walked quite a long way and passed another pub, then up the hill where there were big houses being built. At the top of the hill, they then turned down a lane to Nana Jane's house. On arrival at her house, there were children playing outside, so Gladys said to Teresa, "You play with these little girls for a moment. Mummy won't be long." Teresa played with the little girls, who were from next door. They played out the front of the houses, swinging on the gates and talking. Later, they ran around the back to play hide and seek. Whilst Teresa was hiding, she noticed the back door of Nana Jane's house. Opposite her back gate were trains going past and one of the girls shouted, "Train!" so the girls jumped on the fence and all watched and waved to the train for a moment until the last carriage had passed.

Teresa then ventured in through the back door of Nana Jane's only to hear a lot of arguing and raised voices - they were fighting. Nana Jane was very red in the face, pointing at Gladys and calling her a moll, and saying she was as common as muck. Gladys was just about to go for Jane when she realised Teresa was behind her, watching. It was then that Gladys said to Jane, "You're not worth me wasting my breath. Rot in hell, Jane!" She picked up her handbag, grabbed Teresa's hand, headed for the hallway and left the house. As they walked out of the lane and headed down the road, Gladys noticed Uncle Ben's car driving towards them, then he pulled alongside them next to the pavement. He said hello to Teresa and began a conversation with Gladys. Gladys told Uncle Ben what had happened a few days ago regarding Michael beating her up, and Ben could plainly see her injuries. Gladys went on to tell him it was because of Jane that he had done this, so she had just given Jane a piece of her mind, and if it wasn't for Teresa walking in, she would have hit her. Uncle Ben looked at Gladys and said, "I don't know why she does this. I don't know why she reacts so badly to you at all. And I cannot for the life of me understand why Michael acts like this." Ben then went on to say, "When I see Michael, I will have a word with him. He wasn't brought up like this; he was brought up to respect women, and as for Jane, she must stop interfering in your marriage. Michael is no longer her little boy; he is a fully grown man with responsibilities. I can tell you, Gladys, I am ashamed he did that to you, and I will also be having words with Jane." Uncle Ben, looking very troubled, gave Teresa a kiss, then said goodbye to Gladys as he drove away. Gladys appeared to be happier after speaking to Ben, and Teresa noticed the pace at which they walked back home was much slower. Also, a conversation had taken place between Teresa and Gladys instead of the one-word answers that were being given on the journey to Nana Jane's. Gladys then told Teresa, "Please do not tell your father what Uncle Ben has said because it will make your father very, very mad and we don't want that, do we?" Teresa replied, "I don't like Daddy when he's mad. I won't tell."

Chapter 3

The Ultimatum

Gladys felt she should have told Jane off a lot more than she did, but she couldn't think straight when Teresa walked in and was watching them both. Teresa then started asking Gladys a lot of questions - "Why does Nana Jane hate you? Why does Nana Jane not give us sweets? Nana Jane likes Daddy, doesn't she?" Gladys answered Teresa by telling her, "Not all people get on in life, Teresa, and your Nana Jane and I disagree a lot so that's the end of it." Teresa knew she could ask no more questions but could feel her mother's hands gripping her tighter and tighter. When Gladys finally reached home, she collected Terry and Tabitha from the neighbour next door. Teresa went back outside to play with her friends and told her brother Terry what had gone on at Nana Jane's. Gladys set the table for tea and called the children in to eat, and while they were eating, Michael returned home, hung up his coat and sat down to eat.

All appeared quiet at the table, with everyone eating and nobody saying a word, until Gladys looked across the table at Michael and said, "I've been up to see your mother today, and I gave her a piece of my mind." "What do you mean?" asked Michael as he stood up from the table. Gladys replied, "Just what I said; I gave her a piece of my mind." Michael reached over the table and grabbed Gladys by her throat, bursting the buttons off her blouse. The children jumped off their chairs. Terry grabbed Teresa, and Teresa grabbed Tabitha, and, terrified, they all ran into the living room. The swearing and shouting were as bad as they could get; then they heard the kitchen table, along with their sausage and chips, being thrown to the floor. The screaming continued between the parents when suddenly, Teresa heard her mum say, "I'm only staying because of the kids, but if you visit Jane again, I will leave you." Teresa burst into tears; Tabitha was shaking and she had already wet herself. Terry, trying his hardest to comfort and reassure his sisters, took them upstairs out of the way as the row had now escalated into the living room. Michael put the television on very loud as he continued shouting in the hope that it would drown out the sound of them fighting. With that, the nice neighbour, the one who had given Teresa her cat Fluffy, knocked on the door. When Gladys opened the door, the neighbour asked if everything was okay. She looked at the children, who were then sitting on the stairs, and she told Gladys off, saying, "Fight all you like, but not in front of the children. They are terrified; just look at them!" She then took the children to her house until tensions had calmed down.

Teresa noticed how lovely her house was, with beautiful red curtains, lovely bright rugs, and a polished table with a vase of flowers in the centre. She had a cuckoo clock which had a little bird that came out on the hour saying, "Cuckoo, Cuckoo". Teresa loved her posh house as there was nothing broken. She then heard her parents shouting on the other side of the wall. The neighbour, worried, tried to distract Teresa away from the wall, telling her that her children had grown up and left home. She showed Teresa the photographs of them which were in frames scattered around the house. It was nearing bedtime before Gladys went next door to collect the children. The neighbour had even made food for them, so they were all ready for their tin bath in front of the fire whilst watching television. Gladys thanked her for her kindness and intervention, and then they spoke quietly, not loudly enough for the children to hear. As the children returned to the house with Gladys, they noticed everything was smashed up - the coffee table, the kitchen table, ornaments from the fireplace, and there was a hole in the kitchen door. Gladys skipped their baths and sent all three of them straight to bed.

For weeks, the house was quiet, with Gladys and Michael hardly speaking, and when they did acknowledge each other, it was mainly just by nodding. Teresa, however, was full of questions but getting no answers. Terry was afraid to speak and Tabitha was continually wetting herself. Life was tense in the house, but, as time went by and Michael was not visiting his mother, things slowly seemed to improve. Just as well as it was only weeks until Christmas.

The house was soon decorated and the tree went up, and requests for presents were coming in thick and fast. Teresa desperately wanted a bike, but so did Terry, and Tabitha wanted a doll's house. Expectations were high for the children, and Christmas Eve approached very quickly. Gladys had made her Christmas cake and had pickled her own onions, all the preparations were complete, and the children hung their stockings on the landing stairwell. Terry was in his room, while Teresa and Tabitha, in their single beds, were in their room. All the children had been told not to come out of their rooms or Santa would not come. Teresa, being the mischievous one, encouraged Tabitha to open the bedroom door to see if Santa had been. A reluctant Tabitha did just that but Michael caught her and shouted abruptly, frightening Tabitha into tears saying, "I know Teresa sent you out, so she won't get presents either". Teresa apologised to Tabitha. All the children were very excited about the following day, and Teresa couldn't sleep.

It was still the early hours of the morning when Terry ran into the girls' bedroom shouting, "He's been, he's been! Look, look!" and brought in Tabitha's and Teresa's stockings. There were oranges, apples, nuts and lots of little things like a yoyo, coloured pencils and sweets. The children went running into Michael and Gladys's bedroom to show them what Santa had put in their stockings. Then, their mum and dad went downstairs to light the fire. The children had to wait on the stairs whilst they had their cup of tea and warmed up the living room. "Come on, Mum!" the children would say, very impatiently, just like all children. Finally, after what seemed like forever, they were allowed downstairs. Terry ran into the room first and shouted, "My bike!" Teresa, coming in second, saw that there was no bike for her, so, disappointed, she opened other presents of dolls and toys she didn't want. Tabitha, however, had her doll's house and dolls. Then suddenly, Teresa stood up with her arms folded, started to cry and said, "Where's my bike?" Gladys told her, "You're a girl and Terry is a boy; a bike is more a boy's toy and that's why you haven't got a bike". Teresa sulked all Christmas Day, somewhat spoiling the event, but Terry kept saying to her, "Do you like my bike?" and laughing. Teresa marched up to him and slapped him in the face, then he started shouting, "Tell her, Mum, she's hitting me!" Gladys shouted, "For Christ's sake, Michael, sort her out." Michael took hold of Teresa, telling her she was an ungrateful child and took her to her room. Teresa stood looking out of her bedroom window, elbows on the windowsill and hands on her cheeks, watching other children, including her brother, outside on their new bikes, and youngsters in pedal cars. Teresa shouted out loud to her parents, "I hate you!" From that day on, Teresa felt like the odd one out as Terry was a boy and Tabitha was the youngest. Teresa felt resentment toward both her siblings and had the strength to argue, whereas the others were too scared.

Christmas passed by very quickly, and all the children were growing up fast. Spring passed then summer arrived which meant school broke up for eight weeks. Michael and Gladys planned to take the children to the beach for a caravan holiday. This they did; the caravan was on the sand with lots of others. It had gas lights and bunk beds, and Teresa and her two siblings all played with their buckets and spades in the sand, and went into the water. Teresa, however, was drawn to the water and was very often brought out of it by Michael as she went out too far on many occasions. Teresa enjoyed the sea because as you went further out, the people got smaller like little dots, and it was quiet with just the waves riding over you; this was bliss. One week was planned, but Gladys and Michael made friends with the people in the next caravan and started going out for drinks in the evening. The family were having such a good time that they decided to stay a second week if they could, as their new friends had booked for two weeks. Michael phoned the bank to ask for more money to enable them to stay that extra week. Good times went on again that week as Michael and Gladys took the children to the fair, much to Teresa and Terry's delight, and enjoyed a drink in the evening. However, the good times weren't to stay as on the day of leaving, Teresa caught Terry peeing up against the caravan and told on him. Terry was in trouble and Teresa laughed. The journey home was by train and Tabitha was aggravating the situation between Terry and Teresa, by saying, "You're in trouble, you're in trouble." Terry pinched her and made her cry, so Michael said, "Wait till you get home." Was Tabitha going to be in trouble? No, it was Terry who had a shaking from Gladys. Teresa felt a little bit sorry for him but he shouldn't have peed against the caravan.

Although they were back home now, they were still enjoying the summer months playing outside, when one day, Teresa was told to look after Tabitha as Terry was on his bike up the street. Tabitha had her tin pram and Teresa's friends wanted her to go to their house to play. Teresa knew that if Tabitha was to wet herself, she would be able to take her in, so with that, Teresa told Tabitha to wet herself. Tabitha didn't want to so she started to cry. A neighbour had seen what Teresa was doing and told Gladys. Gladys came out, slapped Teresa and she was dragging her in when the boy next door, Teddy Williams, spat at Gladys in the face. Horrified, Gladys spat right back at him and continued to take Teresa into the house where she had a good slapping. Later that day, a row broke out between Teddy's mother and Gladys over the spitting, fingers pointing at each other and with angry faces and raised voices. Neither woman noticed what was happening around them. Teresa came out to watch what was going on and Teddy, who was older than Teresa, held her hand and took her over the bridge. They were both playing happily on the old train track underneath the bridge, oblivious to all the commotion going on back home regarding them being missing; all the neighbours were out looking. Teresa liked Teddy; he helped her pick daisies in the undergrowth. Over an hour passed, then Teddy and Teresa came back over the bridge. Teresa was very happy with her flowers, which Teddy had helped her pick, then a woman approached them and said, "Home, you two." The woman walked up the street with Teddy and Teresa, and with a big sigh of relief, Gladys told Teresa to come on in, at which point, Teresa said, "I brought you flowers." Gladys took Teresa through the back door into the kitchen where she sat Teresa on the kitchen table and slapped, and slapped, and slapped at her legs. Teresa was crying so hard she could hardly breathe and, being a little bigger now, she tried to get off the table, but Gladys was like something possessed, dragging her up the stairs, still slapping as she threw Teresa onto her bed in her room. Whilst this was going on, Tabitha, who was crouched shaking in the corner, wet herself again. Terry ran upstairs to check on his sister but was told to get down by Gladys. Teresa was sobbing hours later and still in her room when her father Michael brought up jam sandwiches for her and told her she mustn't play with Teddy anymore. Teresa loved Teddy - he was her friend, and she took no notice whatsoever of what her parents said. She carried on playing with Teddy, as did Terry. The summer holidays were soon to be over, and school would soon begin again, so Gladys was busy buying new uniforms in preparation for starting the new term.

September came and Teresa, now seven years old, joined Terry in junior school. Tabitha was four and a half so shortly, she would start infant school. Gladys decided she would get a job when the youngest went to school. Full of ideas, Gladys was planning to alter things in her life, and finally, the day came when Tabitha went to school. Gladys then took a job in a teddy bear factory three evenings a week, meaning Michael would have to look after the children. A month passed and Gladys was enjoying her job when one evening, Michael was throwing a ball at the front of the house when, unfortunately, it hit the bay window smashing the glass. Gladys came home from work; the children were in bed but awake, and Michael decided to blame Terry for the window. Terry was called down from upstairs and he immediately denied this but was then called a liar. Michael shook Terry and told him to tell the truth. Terry, petrified, ran back upstairs screaming and shouting, "I DIDN'T DO IT!" He ran into Teresa's room and asked her if she had seen who did it but Teresa hadn't seen anything. Terry was frightened and confused; why would his dad blame him? Days later, Gladys was outside talking to the neighbours, and one of them told her the truth about the window. She was fuming so went back into the house to confront Michael. Michael was reading the newspaper and smoking his pipe at the kitchen table when Gladys pulled the paper out of his hands and asked for the truth. But Michael was still in full denial over this and called the neighbour a liar, but Gladys says to Michael, "You're the liar, just like you are lying about writing to your mother. Did you not think I would know when strange letters arrived for you? Have you seen her? Tell me; tell me!" Michael grabbed Gladys and slammed her head against the wall several times before kicking her onto the floor. The children ran from all directions upstairs to the landing, afraid to go down, and snuggled close together with Tabitha who was shaking and crying. Gladys shouted to Michael, "Don't shut your eyes because I will get you in your sleep." Michael answered, "She's, my mother". Then Gladys replied, "I'm your wife, and the little ones up there are your children." Michael walked into the hallway, glanced upstairs and saw his children, scared, and huddled together. He then grabbed his coat saying, "I'm off to see my mother; is that alright with you?" and slammed the door on the way out. The children then ran downstairs trying to console their mother. Gladys then told the children to turn on the television. The black and white minstrels were on, followed by Ned the talking horse. They all stayed up late that night.

The following day, Michael hadn't returned home, so Gladys took the children to her adopted mother, the children's nana and grampa down the road. Gladys was talking to Nana and her stepbrother Connor, while Grampa was showing the children how to knit a scarf on nails. He even knitted dogs on them! Also, the children were even allowed sweets from the tin. Gladys then left the house with Uncle Connor, leaving the children with Nana and Grampa. Tabitha was on Grampa's knee, whilst Terry and Teresa, who were waiting for their mother, sat at the table watching out the front window of the house. Hours passed before Gladys came back to take the children home. Terry and Teresa were full of questions like, "Is Daddy coming home?" Gladys replied, "I don't know"; so much uncertainty and no answers. Two days passed before Michael returned home and the arguments recommenced. Gladys told him that he was a mummy's boy, and she couldn't take any more. Gladys then put on her coat and went to work. Terry and Teresa never liked staying with Michael while Gladys worked as they were sent to bed early, but that night, Gladys returned home unexpectedly. An argument broke out about the children being in bed and nothing having been done in the house, when Michael asked her, "Why are you even home?" "I got the sack," replied Gladys. "Why?" asked Michael. "Because they said I kept putting the teddy bears' eyes in crooked," replied Gladys. Michael laughed and laughed! "Oh my god, that's bloody good. No more extra money now then. Hey, I wonder, did the teddy bears see this coming?" he asked. He couldn't stop laughing; in fact, he laughed till he cried. Gladys was furious and asked Michael, "So why don't you take the promotion you were offered then? I will tell you why," she went on to say. "We would have to move, and that means being away from your mother." Michael threw the unwashed dinner plates off the table and went for Gladys. "Oh, here we go again," said Gladys. "Bring it on, mummy's boy!" These words infuriated Michael. The children jumped out of bed and were back on the landing once again. Terry ran down the stairs to protect his mother but got in the way and was thrown across the room, so he then ran outside. Teresa took hold of Tabitha, giving her cuddles whilst waiting for it to stop. An hour passed. Gladys was crying in the kitchen, Michael was outside in his shed, and Teresa and Tabitha ventured downstairs to console their mother. Then, a terrified Terry peeped around the back door, checking it was safe to enter. Gladys checked his body for marks and made sure he was okay. The children were then told to go back to bed as they had school the following morning. Michael came back into the house and spoke under his breath to Gladys, words she could neither understand nor did she want to. She ignored him and went into the living room to watch television. Michael stayed in the kitchen, continuing to mumble under his breath words that sounded like bloody bitch, bloody women, bloody kids.

Chapter 4

The Move

Teresa became a second mum to Tabitha, comforting her, and keeping her safe in the bedroom when raised voices were downstairs. Terry continued to stay on the landing listening to the topics of the rows, which were always money and Michael's mother. Weeks went by and life was normal for the children; normal being the fighting between Mum and Dad. One day, Teresa noticed her cat Fluffy was missing, so she went into the kitchen and asked Gladys, "Where's Fluffy?" Gladys hesitated to answer, so Teresa asked again, "Where's my cat Fluffy? "Gladys replied, "She's gone". Teresa said, "Where's she gone?" Gladys replied, "She shit on Tabitha's pillow; she's gone and won't be back." Teresa burst into tears, slapping at Gladys's legs in fury. "I want my cat, I want my cat, I hate you, I hate you!" Teresa ran upstairs and sobbed her heart out into her pillow. She loved Fluffy; he comforted her and he was hers. Teresa refused to come out of her room at all; she was inconsolable. Her father Michael went upstairs to see her. He sat on her bed beside her and tried to persuade her to eat a jam sandwich, but Teresa refused and told him to go away. Michael told her he would get her another cat, but Teresa wanted her cat Fluffy. As the weeks carried on, time didn't help, as Teresa was still upset. She wouldn't look at her parents, and hated her brother because he kept telling her, "Fluffy's gone". Teresa thumped him on several occasions as she told him, "You don't understand."

Meanwhile, playing outside one day, her brother parked his bike outside the house whilst he went indoors to use the toilet. Teresa couldn't resist taking his bike around the block for a ride. Teresa found this very satisfying and giggled all the way around. She could ride the bike very well but she hated the brakes, so she stopped it by bumping into trees or lampposts. Every time thereafter, if Terry parked his bike, Teresa would steal it and take it around the block. One day, Terry was right behind her when she stole it, screaming at her, "I will kill you! Give me my bike back now!" Teresa pedalled like mad and was glad to see a downhill coming, but she didn't like the brakes, so she jumped off quickly as the bike went off the footpath, into the road, and under the oncoming double-decker bus. Horrified, Terry ran into the house screaming and returned with Michael. Michael retrieved what was now a bent and broken bike and apologised to the bus driver. Michael looked at Teresa and said angrily, "Get into the house. Now." Teresa walked slowly into the house, looking behind her all the way. She knew she was going to get a beating. Then she saw Michael glaring at her, so she ran into the kitchen petrified. Gladys was consoling Terry in the kitchen and said to Teresa, "You should leave his bike alone; I've told you before, and now look what you've done." Michael walked into the house carrying the bike, and said to Teresa, "Come here, you," and with that, he clenched his fists, thumped Teresa in the back, then hit her repeatedly before sending her to her room. Teresa tried to run but was blocked by Terry. Teresa's arms and back were hurting her as she cried, then she shouted, "I hate you all!" and ran to her room. Days passed and Gladys noticed that Teresa's body was covered in bruises. Terry was sorry and was sad to see it. Gladys kept Teresa home from school for a while until the marks and bruising were gone.

Life continued as normal in the household, and money was always a major factor, so Michael decided he would take the promotion. All was well and good, but the promotion meant he would have to travel; therefore, he bought a motorbike to commute. Rows were then about the motorbike; as Michael was too nervous to take a test, he travelled on L-plates until he almost had an accident. One evening, Michael says to Gladys, "They have built new council houses on a new estate near my work if you want to move?" Michael said this as he thought Gladys wouldn't move from her mother down the road. But the unexpected happened and Gladys thought this was a brilliant idea! The rent was cheaper, the bike would go, and the icing on the cake was that he would be away from his mother - win, win. Michael made enquiries and found out they were giving priority to steel-workers who wished to move nearer to work. So, the idea came to fruition, and after arranging new schools for the children, the family moved. Nana

Jane, however, saw straight through Gladys, knowing she was happy moving her son away from her to another town.

The children soon settled into their new schools. Tabitha was growing well, Teresa was being Teresa, and Terry now knew his own mind. They lived in a terraced house and Gladys and Michael were very friendly with the neighbours, each living in each other's houses and going out together socialising. Arguments still happened regularly, but the violence died down for a while. Arrangements were made to visit Nana Jane as a family this time, and they travelled by train which the children always liked. In between visits, Michael would write to his mother regularly, but Gladys knew about it this time. Christmas came and things were looking up as Terry and Teresa were promised a bike each, with Tabitha still wanting a big girl's doll and pram. All was happy that Christmas, with Michael actually stirring the Christmas cake mixture to help with the preparations. Gladys was enjoying her new surroundings and modern house, which was like a horseshoe shape inside; you would enter the hallway through the front door, with the stairs on the right, and carry on into the kitchen. From the kitchen, you could turn left into a dining room, left again into the lounge and another door back into the hallway. The house had three bedrooms and a large modern bathroom. Teresa and Tabitha's room faced the back of the house, whilst Terry's and their parents' rooms faced the front of the house.

Christmas came and Teresa got her bike. She would always be riding around the estate with lots of new friends. Just down the road, there was a river with a bridge over it for the cars, and Teresa and her friends would catch stickleback fish in a net and put them into a jar and take them home. That was until they realised there were too many and they didn't have any room to swim, so they quickly had to get another jar or they would die. On many occasions, Tabitha would be with Teresa as she had to look after her a lot of the time. One day, Teresa was playing with her friends by the river. The bigger boys had tied a tyre onto a rope to enable them to swing over the water. Teresa had done this many times, but Tabitha kept on saying that she wanted a go. Teresa gave in and put Tabitha on the tyre and told her to hold on tight. The boys pushed the tyre a little too hard and, of course, Tabitha fell into the river. Teresa and her friends got Tabitha out and she was hurt, frightened and crying, so Teresa took her home. As they approached the house, Gladys was outside talking to the neighbours. Tabitha ran to her, soaking wet, and said, "Teresa pushed me out of the tyre!" "That's a lie!" Teresa said, and with that, Gladys started attacking Teresa, violently pushing her into the house. She kept on slapping Teresa all the way up the stairs, saying, "Stay in your room; you just cannot be trusted."

The following week, each day when Teresa came home from school, she was not allowed out on her bike, or out with her friends, but was made to play with Tabitha in the house. Teresa became resentful and hated her family, continually telling them she was going to run away. Then one day, her mother packed a carrier bag, made two jam sandwiches, and said to Teresa, "Out you go. If you're going to run away, I will help you." Angrily, she put Teresa's coat on, pushed her out of the door then slammed the door behind her. Being stubborn, Teresa walked down the street. She was not going to show her mother how upset she was, so she waited until she was out of sight and then cried, feeling like she was never wanted, and was again the least favourite; the odd one out. "I wish I'd brought my bike," thought Teresa. "I could go for miles, and they would never find me, and I would never have to speak to Tabitha again, the liar." She then met up with friends and told them she couldn't go home. One boy offered her his garden shed, but Daisy, one of her friends, said, "Come home with me. My mum won't mind; she's mostly in the pub so she won't know anyway."

Hours passed until Michael was made to go and look for her. Michael found her on a wall by the shops with her friends and told her she must be better behaved and to let this be a lesson to her. Teresa told her father that she had only helped Tabitha into the tyre; it was the big boys who had pushed her. Michael answered saying, "You shouldn't have put her in the tyre in the first place as she's too young for that sort of fun." "Will you tell Mum then? She doesn't believe me, and I want to go out on my bike," said Teresa. Michael said, "Yes, I will tell your mother and everything will be okay". He took her hand and led her home. Teresa walked slowly to the house and on entering, noticed that Gladys wasn't there; she was round at the neighbour's house next door. Gladys appeared to always be round at the neighbour's house (Janet, her new best friend), and this meant Teresa was made to do the washing up, help around the house and do chores whilst Terry never had to do anything. "Tabitha is too young," Gladys would say, "and Terry is a boy; they don't do chores." Teresa went straight up the stairs to her room and never spoke to Tabitha. Tabitha tried to talk to Teresa, telling her, "Mum said to tell you to do the washing up when you came home." Teresa ignored what she said, nor did she go back downstairs to wash up. "That isn't fair," thought Teresa, feeling very angry.

So, one day, a few weeks later, when Gladys returned from Janet's house next door, she noticed Teresa had not dried the dishes, so she called Teresa down from upstairs and was telling her off, when Teresa swore at her, stuck her tongue out and ran. Gladys gave chase. Teresa ran through the dining room, through to the lounge and Gladys took off her slipper to throw at Teresa. Teresa ducked but Terry opened the door and the slipper hit him straight in the head. Gladys apologised to Terry but sent Teresa to her room saying, "Get out of my sight!" The following day being a Friday, after school, the family were due to visit Nana Jane, and Terry was staying with her for the weekend. This was the first time anyone had stayed at Nana Jane's. Terry did enjoy his weekend stay, and it wasn't long before it was time to visit again. Terry again was staying for the weekend, but he wanted Teresa to stay with him this time. Teresa asked, "What's it like staying at Nana Jane's house?" "It's good," said Terry. "I have friends there now as well." Teresa asked if she could stay the weekend with Terry at Nana Jane's and Michael and Gladys agreed. Teresa was to stay in the front bedroom, while Terry would stay in the back bedroom. On arrival, Teresa noticed Nana Jane had a front room which was called the best room, and there were tall cabinets made of wood in there which were full of tins of fruit and other foods. The room had a big bay window and, on the windowsills, stood large China ornaments. There were posh chairs with large cushions on them, plus the room smelt of polish and the wood did shine. She continued looking around the house whilst the adults talked. A couple of hours later, she said her goodbyes to the family as they left to return home. It was approaching nine o'clock and Uncle Ben said it was time for bed, so both Terry and Teresa made their way upstairs to their rooms. As she lay in bed, she noticed everything was so quiet, not a sound; "not like living on an estate," she thought. Soon, she fell fast asleep, as did Terry.

The following morning, she was awoken by the sun shining through the curtains into her room. She looked at the time; it was only six-thirty in the morning, so she lay there for a while listening to the birds chirping in the trees. Somehow, she felt different; she felt a sort of happiness. She got out of her very comfortable double bed and walked over to the window to open her curtains. Not only could she hear the birds but she could actually see them. Teresa watched in amazement for a while then decided to wash, clean her teeth, and get dressed. It wasn't until she ventured downstairs that she realised that after her breakfast, she must dust the furniture. "You must do this whilst Nana runs the hoover around," Terry told her, "and whilst I go out to play." This Teresa did, although she did feel misled into staying. Besides, Nana Jane frightened Teresa by saying, "This hoover will know if you don't dust properly, and it has a big enough bag to suck you up!" Teresa was scared as the bag really did blow up. After the work was done, Nana Jane let Teresa put lipstick and a little powder on as she was taking her to town, and Terry could stay with his friends. Even though Uncle Ben had a car, they walked into town. Ben didn't talk very much but gave Terry and Teresa money. Nana Jane and Teresa went into a grocer's shop, where Nana Jane told Teresa to sit on the high stool in front of the counter whilst she gave her order to the shopkeeper. The shop had a very strong smell of ground coffee. Teresa was told by Nana Jane that she was allowed a chocolate bar and to let the lady know which one she wanted. After that, they started the journey back home, looking in different shops on the way, whilst Teresa ate her bar of chocolate. She remembered the free house pub as she passed it, and her mother telling her it was not a house. Terry was still out playing with his friends when Nana Jane and Teresa arrived back at the house. Later, Nana Jane called him in for his tea. Terry and Teresa had a good posh meal; salmon sandwiches, followed by fruit and custard for afters - they never had afters at home ever. The following day, Teresa had to dust once again, but later decided to go out to play with the girls next door. She had lots of fun and Terry was enjoying himself train-spotting, and writing down the names, makes, and models of the different trains that passed at the back of Nana's house. Later that evening, their parents and Tabitha came and stayed for about an hour talking to Uncle Ben and Nana Jane. They then took Terry and Teresa back home. Teresa and Terry noticed that Gladys only ever spoke to Uncle Ben but didn't know why that was.

Several weeks later, Terry said to Teresa, "Are you coming to stay with

Nana Jane this weekend?" Teresa replied, "No." Terry said, "You must, please, aww, please stay." Teresa asked him why. "Because I have to help Nana Jane with the dusting, but if you're there, I don't have to." Teresa said, "I'm never staying at Nana's again. Go on your own!" This resulted in neither sibling wanting to stay again, and all the family thinking that Teresa was selfish. Michael also blamed Gladys, as he thought she had turned the children against his mother, and for not trying hard enough to persuade Terry and Teresa to stay. A massive row broke out because nobody wanted to visit Nana Jane, who would be expecting one if not two of the children to stay, resulting in Michael visiting his mother completely on his own. It was very late in the evening before Michael returned home; he had obviously taken the last train back. On his return, the children were woken by screaming and shouting, so, once again, they jumped out of bed, and were listening at the top of the stairs. The last thing they heard was Michael saying to Gladys, "Look what you made me do now! You bring this out in me all the time; what's the matter with you, woman?"

The following morning, Gladys had her head bandaged as it was bleeding. She was preparing breakfast when the children asked if she was alright. Gladys couldn't help herself; "Your father has visited his mother again, hasn't he?" The children just looked at each other with a worried look and proceeded on to school. Hours later, the children returned home from school only to find that Gladys wasn't there. She was next door talking to Janet, who had taken her to hospital that day to get some treatment for her head as she needed to have stitches. Michael returned home and neither were talking to each other. Tensions were high, so all the children knew it was best to go out and play. Terry went with his friends, and Teresa and Tabitha went with Teresa's friends, who then decided to go scrumping apples. Some of the girls knew exactly where to go, according to Teresa's friend Jackie, so off they all went with Jackie in the lead. The three girls were chuckling as they walked up a long narrow lane. Teresa and Tabitha had identical flowery red dresses on which weren't really climbing attire. They came across massive green gates which Jackie opened slowly as they creaked. They walked through several trees, which some of their friends started swinging on, before coming to the apple tree. Tabitha was elated as some of the apples were in her reach and rosy red. The girls realised they had nothing to put the apples in, so they lifted their dresses in order to make a bag. The two dresses were as full as could be, so they then started to leave the orchard, giggling away, as they were very pleased with their achievement. Sadly, they were heard, and a man with a face as red as the apples gave chase swinging something like a walking stick. The girls ran away, but the man knew Jackie's parents and shouted, "I know your father, Jackie, and I am going to tell him what you have stolen." He followed the girls and headed directly to Jackie's house; he then told her father what she had done. Later, Jackie's dad, who lived opposite, told Michael. Michael was furious. He went into the house and grabbed hold of Teresa, taking her to the floor, kicking and kicking at her legs and back. Teresa was screaming; she held her arms over her head in order to protect her head and face, and with that, Gladys pushed Michael off Teresa and took a beating herself. Meanwhile, Terry was very scared at seeing his mother and Teresa being beaten, so he ran as fast as he could out of the house. Tabitha was in hysterics as she watched her sister curled up in a ball unable to move. Michael put his coat on and left the house. Unable to move, Teresa cried out to her mother for help. Gladys helped Teresa to the couch. Gladys, bleeding herself, went next door for help.

Janet looked at Teresa's legs and said, "We should check he hasn't broken her legs. Looking at her injuries, she needs a doctor." Gladys replied, "No doctor! I will bandage them and see how she goes." Both Gladys and Janet helped Teresa upstairs to rest, giving her pain relief, and putting cold bandages around her legs to bring the swelling down. They both then continue downstairs. Tabitha stayed on the bed with Teresa until Gladys put her into her own bed later. Meanwhile, Janet's husband Jack was out looking for Terry. Hours passed and still in shock, Janet asked Gladys, "How could he do this?" Gladys replied, "It's his mother. As I told you before, he has a mother complex and sadly, this time, he took it out on Teresa. He saw a reason to let his anger out and did just that." She then went on to say, "Teresa is his favourite, so he is going to feel it; he will be riddled with guilt and remorse." Meanwhile, worry over Terry was escalating as the night drew in. Jack was still looking but could not find him, and Jack's children, who were teenagers, were also searching. Hours passed; Janet was still comforting Gladys when they suddenly thought to maybe try the train station. That was the only real journey Terry knew. Fortunately, Jack saw Terry, a very frightened young boy who didn't want to go home, trying to board a train. The station master was about to call the police as Terry wouldn't talk to him, but he then made sure that Terry knew Jack. Terry nodded when asked if he knew him, and he then left the platform with Jack. They both went into a nearby café where Jack was hoping to calm him down and hopefully reassure him. But how could he do that? When he asked if Terry was okay, the boy got upset, telling all to Jack; how he was afraid of his father, thinking his dad had killed his sister. Jack told him that everything was fine - his sister wasn't dead, but she was badly hurt. Jack asked him if he would like to see his car. Terry agreed and got into the car; it was a Morris Minor, a car he liked. Jack watched Terry carefully and thought to himself, "He is obviously worried about his sister and mother but thought he would be the next, that's why he ran," as he had previously said this to Jack. "I really don't wish to go back home ever," Terry said to Jack. Jack wasn't sure what he could say or do, but gave him a bar of chocolate, and told him If he felt like running again, just to run into his house next door, as he would be safe there.

While Jack was away comforting Terry, Michael came back and told Janet to leave. Janet said, "What kind of a monster are you, to hurt your child and your wife?" Michael said, "So what? At least I don't cheat on her. Your husband goes with a lot of women when we go out for a drink; oh yes, he's quite the lady's man, so he's not so perfect now, is he?" Janet ran out of the house crying. Gladys stood up and said to Michael, "You are a monster, and now you have caused a lot of trouble for Janet, Jack, and their family. Just how far will you go? Jack is out looking for your son; you're despicable!" She glared at him as she turned and left the room.

Approximately an hour later, Jack called in with Terry. At this point, Michael was in the bathroom behind a locked door, so Gladys thanked him sincerely, as she was so pleased and relieved that her son was safe and well. Then, she said, "Jack, you need to go home - he has upset Janet". "What do you mean?" Jack demanded, but Gladys simply said, "I'm truly sorry, Jack," and shut the door. Gladys settled Terry down in bed saying, "We will talk in the morning". Then all Gladys could hear was rowing next door, then Jack came banging on her front door, shouting at the top of his voice, "Michael, get out here now!" and swearing he was going to kill him. Meanwhile, Michael was pleading with Gladys, "Don't open the door; please, don't open the door." Gladys replied, "Why the hell shouldn't I, Michael? Why the hell shouldn't I?" Jack left the front door and went back out in his car. Michael, still hiding behind a locked door, broke down and cried like a baby. Gladys left him there and decided to go to bed, checking on Teresa first before settling down herself.

The next day, the family were all shaken up and very unhappy. Michael was mumbling to himself, walking around the house not knowing what to do. Gladys felt emotionally broken; she decided no school for the children, and no work for Michael, so Michael went to the phone box down the road and called in sick. Gladys went next door and apologised to her friend for Michael's behaviour. Janet said to Gladys, "He's gone, Gladys, I can't look at him. I threw him out." Janet's two children, Peter and Susan, were comforting her on the settee and didn't say a word to Gladys, but they looked at her in such a way as to say it was her fault, as they adored their father. Gladys left the house feeling unwelcome and sad, so she returned home. Teresa, still in her bed, had a visit from her father, who was crying, apologetic and said, "I will never hurt you again. I love you, your brother, and your sister." Teresa wouldn't say a word; in fact, she felt very nervous and vulnerable as she knew she couldn't run. He went to take Tabitha's hand to take her downstairs, but she cried and pulled away. Tabitha wanted to stay with her sister.

The house remained very quiet and nobody seemed to go anywhere or do anything except for Michael. He made an appointment to see his doctor later that day where he was diagnosed as having a nervous breakdown, Michael was given tablets to help calm his nerves. As the days continued, Teresa was limping around with her legs bandaged. Friends knocked at the door to see if she was going out to play, but they were all sent away by Gladys, who told them, "Teresa is ill, so she can't come out to play today." Tabitha became clingy to Teresa and her mum, and, as she was still frightened of her father Michael, she would hide behind Teresa most of the time. Terry, however, was bought a record player to keep him occupied in the house, as none of the children were allowed outside. Weeks later, Gladys and Michael were talking quietly in the lounge whilst smoking and having a cup of tea. Terry told Teresa they were planning a move, as he had been listening on the stairs. Teresa got upset as she liked her school and her friends, and she was going to play the lead role in a school play called Alison's Christmas Party.

Teresa was playing Alison; therefore, she didn't want to leave. The teachers had previously told Gladys and Michael that Teresa was very talented and loved the stage, and they recommended drama school for her. Teresa also excelled in maths and English, and always had good grades and reports. Terry's reports were also good, but Tabitha was falling behind which was a cause for concern. Even Teresa had noticed she wouldn't leave her side or make her own friends. She wouldn't mix with others at all. Two weeks later, only Terry and Tabitha returned to school and they were told not to tell anyone about Teresa's beating by her father. It was another two weeks after that before Teresa returned to school. This was because Teresa's legs were so badly bruised that they had to wait until all above-knee bruising had gone as her long white socks would cover below the knee. However, Michael was still not in work, and as Christmas approached, tensions were rising as raised voices returned, with money being the cause.

Teresa did her Christmas school play, and Christmas Eve was here again. The very same pattern occurred on Christmas Day - the children were to wait on the stairs whilst Mum and Dad drank a cup of tea and warmed the house. Three excited children then ran down to open their presents; their piles were very small; small gifts for each. Teresa had a Cinderella watch which was attached to a china model of Cinderella, Tabitha had yet more dolls, and Terry had writing sets and records for his record player. Teresa's favourite present was her diary with a golden pen and a lock. "I can write my secrets in here," she thought, "and nobody will see it; I can lock it up." That year, the snow was very deep, so they were all blocked in their houses, and no schools were open due to the frozen pipes in the outside toilets. The children enjoyed the snow, playing and building snowmen and making snow angels with their friends. Sometimes, snowball fights got a little out of control as laughter and wickedness took over, with windows and innocent passers-by being hit, but all was well and as normal as a child's life should be.

In the meantime, Gladys and Michael were planning a move back home and would live back near Nana Jane's house again. Nana Jane had got them a flat in the town centre to help them get back onto the council housing list. Nana Jane was glad to see her son was coming back home. Nana Price and Grampa were very excited also, as they missed their grandchildren calling in for sweets, and were very worried about Gladys. A few weeks later, Michael had arranged to have his old job back, still with the steelworks, but it was to be a demoted position, which was better for him as the promoted job was much more stressful which didn't help with his nerves, and may have been a factor in his behaviour. Whilst telling the children one evening, there was a mixed response. Terry was very happy, as he only had a few months before going to the all-boys comprehensive, Tabitha was not far off junior school, and Teresa would be going into the last year of juniors. Teresa folded her arms and stamped her feet, insisting she wasn't moving; she liked her teachers, friends, and school. Michael took her aside and promised her things would be better going back to her hometown. "If you want to, you can have another cat," he promised. Open to bribery, Teresa agreed but was still not very happy. When school re-opened, she took her note into school explaining the move to her teacher. There were tears in her eyes, as this particular teacher had always guessed that things weren't alright at home, and always gave Teresa a little more attention than her other pupils. Teresa told her best friends, as did Tabitha. A week before the move, the children left school to help with packing, and adjust to the changes. Then, the day finally came for the move and the big removal van pulled up outside the house. All the children were helping to put boxes into the van when they saw Janet from next door approaching Gladys. She cried and hugged Gladys, and they were both emotional. Janet then walked over to Teresa, hugged her, and whispered in her ear, "I'm going to miss you, my darling, but just remember where I am if you need me. Promise me, Teresa, yes?" Teresa hugged her back. "I promise," replied Teresa.

With the house all packed up and the contents put into the removal van, so began the journey back home, as Gladys and Michael called it. During the journey, Teresa thought long and hard about Janet, and how she was going to miss her, but how could she keep her promise when she had no means of getting to her? Still, she was happy that Janet and Jack were together once again, even if they never bothered with her father Michael ever again. The journey didn't seem to take very long, or was it because Teresa was thinking about things and changes once again? Who knew what destiny lay ahead?

The lorry stopped in the middle of the town, holding up all the traffic. Horns were beeping, and people shouting, but it made no difference to the removal men - they just carried on unloading the furniture. Michael was shouting at the children, "Carry what you can into the flat and leave them on the lower level, then I will take them up later. Come on, kids, as fast as you can." Cars and vans continued to beep, but the lorry never moved until all the furniture was safely delivered into the flat. Michael paid and thanked them, then began the hard and strenuous work of getting lots of boxes to the upper floors, helped by all the family, of course.

Chapter 5

The Return of the Thomas Family

The flat was huge, much bigger for them than the homes they'd had before, and right in the middle of town. Terry and Teresa were excited running up and down the several staircases, looking through the old sash-type windows which would only open a little bit; they thought this was great. There were all the shops, a small garden out the back, and even a basement which was too scary to investigate. Everything was looking up for them as they sorted their bedrooms out and explored the surroundings. The front door to the flat opened out onto the main street of town by the traffic lights, so they were warned to be very careful, and not to get run over as it was always extremely busy.

However, a few weeks later, Gladys had news that her mother, Nana Price, had died and Grampa Price had to go into hospital as he was very ill. With all this happening, everything was calm between Michael and Gladys, and, along with her brother Connor, she arranged their mother's funeral. Grampa Price was going to live with Connor and May when he came out of hospital. After her mother's funeral, the children were sent to their new schools. All siblings appeared settled in school apart from Teresa. Teresa started fighting in school, and name-calling both at school and at home with her siblings. She was struggling with the upheaval of her life in general, and this school wasn't the same as her last school. Michael tried to settle her by getting her the cat he had promised. Teresa loved animals and this cat was a little girl, a tortoiseshell colour as they are known. Teresa immediately named her Twinkie like the stars twinkling in the sky. Teresa then settled down a little in school, and it wasn't long before the summer holidays were here, which meant school broke up for eight weeks, however, the family had no holiday again this year as once again, money was too tight. September was approaching and that meant Teresa would lose her brother Terry in junior school, as he was heading for the all-boys comprehensive school. She had never liked her new junior school and couldn't wait to leave; the girls weren't as nice as in her last school although she still made friends. One of her friends just lived with her dad; she had no mother, she told Teresa. "They fought and split up." Teresa seemed very interested in this because she was very happy, and always carried lots of money, so this made Teresa think, "Maybe my parents will split up," half-hoping they would. Teresa was learning about life, so that night, Teresa asked her father if she could have pocket money. Michael said, "Don't be so soft; where do you think I can get that?" Teresa replied, "Your job". Michael turned and clipped Teresa around the head and sent her into the other room for dinner. Teresa, sulking as usual, said, "It's not fair; my friends have pocket money". With that, Gladys said, "Maybe you should go and live with your Nana Jane. After all, you are just like her". Tabitha chirped up, "Is Teresa going to live with Nana Jane?" Michael said, "No, she isn't. Nana Jane just thought it would be nice. But your mother said no." Terry then said, "Well, I'm not going to live at Nana Jane's," then Michael said, "Why do you not like Nana Jane?" He then turned to Gladys and said, "Look what you've started. You have turned them against my mother!" Gladys replied, "Oh, here we go again. Your bloody mother!" Michael just looked at everyone and walked out of the room, slamming the door.

Over the following weeks, Gladys was back and forth to the housing office to chase up a council house for the family because the flat was far too big. She found it hard to heat and very expensive with the rent. Michael continued taking tablets for his nerves, and Gladys carried on as best she could, but undoubtedly, very unhappy and frustrated with her life, especially the bit about the mother-in-law, whom she hated with a vengeance. Gladys would always say, "She will live to be a hundred and receive a telegram from the queen."

In the meantime, Terry and Teresa would have fun dropping pieces of bread, or anything else they could find, on people's heads on the pavement below. Then they would duck when they looked up to see what had hit them. They could never contain their laughter as they thought it was so funny until they got caught out by their mother Gladys. Both were sent to their rooms and Gladys locked Teresa's door. Teresa didn't like being locked in, so she banged the door, continually screaming and shouting. She had no reaction from Gladys, so Teresa thought she had left her locked in and gone out. Frustrated, Teresa made a fist and pushed it through the front bedroom window. Her thumb and hand were bleeding badly. Her temper had got the better of her. She was retaliating and fighting back the only way she knew how. Gladys heard the window breaking and rushed to Teresa's room and wrapped her hand in a towel. Terry and Tabitha looked on in shock as they wouldn't dream of doing a thing like that; they would both be too scared. But Teresa? No, her spirit was harder to break than her siblings, and she stood up for herself. Hospital attention was needed for her hand, and stitches were put in her thumb, Teresa just cried. Gladys explained to the nurse that she had done it intentionally and she didn't know what to do with her. On the way home from hospital with her hand and thumb bandaged, Gladys asked, "Why do you misbehave all the time?" Teresa, being cheeky, replied, "Why do you and Dad always fight? Why do I have to do everything? Why did you sell my bike?" Gladys replied, "Your bike was too small for you, and you must understand your father is ill, that's why he takes tablets". When they returned home, Tabitha cried when she saw her sister bandaged up as she had seen the blood and thought she was going to die. Terry, on the other hand, just smirked and said, "That showed them not to lock you in," feeling very pleased with his sister as she'd had the guts to do that, which he never would. Teresa sat on the settee, with her cat Twinkie as usual, watching TV when a row broke out in the kitchen between Michael and Gladys again, this time over Teresa's actions and misbehaviour. Michael said, "You should never have sold her bike". Gladys replied, "If you had been working at the time, I wouldn't have had to sell the bike!" Michael rapidly replied, "You never sold Terry's, did you? It's always Teresa's, isn't it?" Gladys walked into the television room and just shook her head directly at Teresa saying, "Now look what you have done! Go to bed and get out of my sight." This she did taking her cat with her.

A month went by until payday came round for Michael, and on his list was a bike for Teresa. It wasn't a new one like before, but a second-hand one with a carry basket on the front. Teresa was delighted because, at the back of the flat, there were several lanes in which she could ride. Terry, however, was jealous and poked fun at the bike whilst Tabitha rode on the back with her having lots of fun and time out with Teresa. Soon after, the day finally came when the family were allocated a council house. It was in a different part of the estate they had originally come from. This house was at the top of the estate, almost opposite the infant school Teresa had attended. The house was right on a corner with a very large lawned garden at the front as well as out the back, plus a handy bus stop just down the road. Michael and Gladys spent hours painting and wallpapering and making it home, buying brand new furniture, plus a large gramophone, which played records as well as the radio, and new curtains, which had to be private and non-see-through when it was dark, especially if the lights were on in the house. Sometimes, Gladys would send the children outside just to check that they couldn't see in. They also bought brand-new red swirly fitted carpets for the rooms and new linoleum for the kitchen. The house was fresh and new, and Teresa, just like Terry, soon made friends and both were happier there than in the flat; plus, they weren't in a different town.

Twinkie the cat gave birth to six kittens on Teresa's bed. That was beyond a surprise. She found a box and lined it with old towels, cutting one side down for Twinkie to get in and the kittens, when bigger, to get out. My, how she loved them all, and her father Michael was pleased to see Teresa smiling again. Life was on the up for Teresa who was much happier in herself and her surroundings. Each day after school, she would run home to check on her new cat family, while she still couldn't understand how the kittens were all different colours. Their eyes were now open and all they did was slide along the box looking to feed from Twinkie and meowing non-stop. One kitten was ginger, another two were tortoiseshell, one ginger and white, and two black and white. Teresa was continually picking up the kittens and stroking Twinkie. She would stay there looking at them for hours, watching their behaviour and becoming very attached to all of them. Tabitha was also attached to and loved the ginger one, but Terry wasn't interested; he was focusing on his new school and felt like he was the big boy in his cap and uniform. The uniform was navy with long trousers in winter and short trousers in the summer. The tie made him feel all grown up, and it did suit him, what with a white shirt and blazer and the school's name embroidered on the pocket of the blazer and his cap. Teresa knew it wouldn't be long until she was in uniform in the all-girls school when the following term ended. She didn't like the school she was in now but did like her friends.

Chapter 6

The Breakdown

Life carried on happily for the family until Tabitha told her big sister she was being bullied. Teresa replied, "Did you tell Mum?" Tabitha replied, "Yes, I did, and she said to ignore her." Tabitha went on to say the girl's name was Pamela, and she had started pushing her around and making her cry. Pamela was older than Tabitha, so Teresa assumed it was the Pamela she had fallen out with weeks before. Teresa turned to Tabitha and said, "Don't worry, I will get her." Returning to school the following day, Tabitha couldn't find Pamela, and Teresa thought that perhaps she wasn't in school, however, later, Tabitha, upset and crying, pointed her out in the big girls' class, but Teresa could only see the back of her as they were all lined up ready to go back into class. Teresa watched to see which classroom they went into and followed them. To her surprise, there she was. It was the Pamela she had fallen out with. Teresa asked Pamela, "Have you been bullying my sister?" Pamela said, "No, I haven't, so get lost." With that, Teresa punched Pamela in the face and pushed her over the desk. The class was watching, cheering Teresa on, as Pamela was a bully in school and not many liked her at all. Pamela got up holding her mouth, and blood was seeping through her fingers. With that, Teresa left before the teacher came in, shouting to Pamela, "Touch her again and I'll kill you". Teresa went to her class, but she wasn't there long before the headmaster came in and called her to the office. The headmaster, Mr James, told Teresa that violence wasn't acceptable in his school and Teresa got the cane, but she didn't care as she lived with a bully and hated them. And after all, she was only defending her sister. During the return home, Teresa and Tabitha decided not to tell their parents for fear of Teresa getting into more trouble.

The following day being a Saturday, there was no school. The sun was shining and Teresa and Tabitha were playing with friends in the street; they were skipping, and playing jacks until Teresa was called into the house from outside. In the house, her mother had a visitor, a woman she apparently knew; the woman was very short and wore a headscarf. She turned out to be Pamela's mother, Mrs Stone. The secret was out, Teresa just knew. Teresa was accused of hitting two front teeth out of Pamela's mouth, and Pamela's mother was telling Gladys that she needed to punish Teresa for such dreadful behaviour, but Teresa, in her defence, told them she'd had the cane, and anyway, Pamela had been bullying Tabitha. "That's outrageous," Mrs Stone replied. "Pamela would never bully anyone." And with that, Tabitha was called into the room. Gladys said, "We will sort this out now". She then asked Tabitha if Pamela was bullying her. Tabitha replied, "Yes, I told you before, Mum". A very angry Mrs Stone left the house and returned with Pamela. Gladys called Tabitha back in and asked her again; "Did Pamela bully you?" Tabitha replied, "No, not her, another Pamela". Teresa was in big trouble. She'd hit the wrong Pamela. Teresa, for once, had no words. Gladys tried to calm the situation and put the kettle on while Mrs Stone and her had a talk. Teresa was told she couldn't go out after school for two weeks and made her apologise and make friends with Pamela. This Teresa did as she did feel awful over the mix-up. Gladys told her she would visit the school about the other Pamela on Monday.

When the girls returned to school, word got around the classes about what Teresa had done for her sister, and, in a way, it did some good as no one would hurt Tabitha anymore. Girls who were being bullied went to Teresa and told her, and all Teresa had to do to the bullies was have a word; a nice threatening word always did the trick. Mrs Stone (Maisie) and Gladys became close friends after the incident, and Pamela and Teresa, along with Tabitha, walked to school together and played together. Mrs Stone became someone whom Gladys would confide in and she regularly visited the house or they would go shopping together.

As the weeks went on, the kittens were getting bigger and were all over the house. So, Michael told Teresa to take them to the RSPCA van, which visited on a Tuesday by the shops, as they would then have a nice home. Teresa put a cardboard box lined with their blanket in the basket of her bike to transport the kittens to the shops. Teresa wanted to keep some, if not all, but her father told her, "If you keep Twinkie's kittens, Twinkie will leave home". Teresa didn't want that, so she rode her bike down to the shops and handed over six healthy kittens to the man, and he assured her they would go to nice homes. However, days passed and Twinkie was looking for her kittens. This upset Teresa but Michael told her this would pass and it did; Twinkie was happy again.

One day, Mrs Stone's husband came to the house to pick up his wife. He had a black car, a Volkswagen Beetle. Michael was talking to him and decided he was going to take driving lessons, and, within a week, Michael had bought a car. It was a blue one and a different shape from Mr Stone's car. His was a Triumph Herald. Gladys didn't like the idea of a car because of his nerves, therefore, she worried. Michael bought the car with money he borrowed from Nana Jane. This didn't sit well with Gladys at all. She thought Jane was interfering again, but there was nothing she could do. Michael said to Gladys, "Dan is going to teach me; he will sit beside me, and it isn't going to cost a penny". Gladys replied, "What about your nerves?" Michael got angry, saying, "Stop putting me down. I can do it; life will be better for us with the car". Gladys replied, "We will see. We will see". She was totally unconvinced.

Gladys started going out quite often with Maisie, or Mrs Stone as Teresa knew her. Gladys would dress up very smartly with her high heels that made a clip-clop sound, hair done, nice clothes and handbags. She wore make-up with bright red lipstick, which Teresa hated as she would kiss her and try to rub it off with a handkerchief. They would go to bingo regularly and come home late, the children being left with Michael. A few weeks passed and Michael was driving with Dan beside him when a near accident occurred, and Dan shouted at Michael. Michael had pulled the steering wheel right off as he was holding it so tight. He was very nervous of the road and nearly killed himself and Dan.

Rows started again over the car, with Gladys saying, "Me and the kids will never get in a car with you driving; I told you so." Michael lashed out again at Gladys, and Terry jumped on Michael saying, "Leave her alone!" Michael turned on him and viciously kicked him to the floor. Gladys shouted, "Leave him alone! You're not going to hurt him. It's right what I say - you take things out on the children - pick on me, you coward. Come on, you only hit women and children." Michael was shocked and walked out of the house. He was furious. Teresa and Tabitha came in from outside and saw furniture upside down and Gladys comforting Terry. He was very upset and lifted his top to reveal big red marks. Gladys also had a bleeding lip. Michael never came home that night. Next morning, Teresa and Tabitha were sent to school, but Terry was kept home because of his injuries. Gladys didn't worry about where Michael was as she knew he would be at his mother's house. Teresa and Tabitha returned from school that afternoon and there was still no sign of Michael. They had their tea and Tabitha went outside to play whilst Teresa went to her room and put her music on. She was growing up fast - pop posters on the wall on her side of the bedroom- the Bee-Gees, the Beetles, Cliff Richard, and Tom Jones. She was also becoming very conscious of what she wore and how she looked. She would sing along pretending her hairbrush was a microphone whilst brushing her long dark hair. She longed for the day she could wear high heels and put make-up on. Time wasn't going fast enough for her. As she lay in bed, she listened to the ladies' heels clip-clopping as they walked past the house late at night, but she knew she would soon be starting the comprehensive all-girls school.

Tabitha didn't like the idea of being alone and maybe unprotected, as Teresa always looked after her. Terry started to think he could protect his siblings and his mother, but he was no match for Michael. Terry promised Teresa that he would stop his father from ever hurting her again. He felt he was a man now, but he wasn't yet; he was still a boy in his teenage years, hormones all over the place. Bedtime came at 7:30 for Tabitha, 8:30 for Teresa and 9:00 for Terry, as he was the eldest.

Morning came, and again, no sign of Michael. The children made their way to school. Maisie came to keep Gladys company for the day, shopping and talking for hours; the time always seemed to go fast, and it wasn't long before Pamela, Teresa, Tabitha and Terry were back home from school. Same routine as always - they had their tea and went to their rooms. Teresa would play her music, Terry would be in his room, and Tabitha dancing, or out playing. All the children were doing their own thing, as you would say, when Michael suddenly came up the stairs. He barged into Teresa's room, went straight to her large, heavy box-sized radio and unplugged it, then heaved it down the stairs. Teresa, in hysterics, started slapping Michael and saying, "Don't do that; you'll break it!" With that, he pushed Teresa down after it. She fell several steps, and, as she was hurting, she swore at Michael and said, "I'm going to smash up everything you have. I hate you! Come here, because I'm going to kill you!" Michael, full of rage, wasn't expecting a reaction like that from Teresa. He thought the way she spoke to him was disrespectful and his anger grew stronger, so he replied, "Wait there because I'm coming to kill you; you won't get up this time." Teresa, crying, ran through the hallway, through the dining room and into the kitchen. Michael was right behind her so Teresa was cornered. As Michael came face to face with her, she raised her hand and slapped his cheek. His hand went up and he shouted, "No kid of mine slaps me!" As he went to slap Teresa, Gladys got in the way, pushing him back and saying, "Your children are growing up and they're not going to stand for this anymore. Can't you see that? And I'm not going to stay, because my children are now getting in the way of you hitting me!" With that, Michael stopped. He slid down the wall, crying. He cried like a baby saying, "What's wrong with me?" Teresa was immediately sent into the living room by Gladys.

Gladys put the kettle on. All three children listened at the door whilst Gladys was telling him he needed help from the doctor. Teresa heard him say, "I would have killed her this time, wouldn't I?" Gladys replied, "Yes." Later, after listening to Gladys, Michael agreed to get help.

Teresa's radio was destroyed. She had only just got it as her parents had given it to her when they bought the gramophone, so Terry said if she wanted, she could borrow his record player. Once again, Teresa was going to bed sore, and afraid of more rows that may occur that night. Teresa slept very lightly, hearing every creak there was to hear. The next morning, all the children attended school, and all was quiet when they left. However, Tabitha was crying in school and the teacher asked what was troubling her. She was too scared to say, so the teacher called Teresa and asked her, but Teresa told the teacher that Tabitha wouldn't say. Teresa settled her down with a drink until she felt better. On the way home, Teresa and Tabitha were talking about the night before, wondering how it would be today. Then Teresa noticed police vans and an ambulance outside their house. They were afraid of the police as they were always told that if you bring the police to the house, you're in the worst trouble ever. Lots of neighbours were gathered around the house with folded arms and gossiping about the family, waiting for news and activity, smoking cigarettes, and wearing long pinafores and headscarves. Some were staring at them as they approached and they heard one say, "Here they come; here they come". Teresa wondered if the police were there for them and she was very frightened.

Out of nowhere, Maisie grabbed them and said, "Sorry, girls, you can't go into your house". "Why?" Teresa shouted. Maisie then said to them both, "Your mother will explain shortly". They sat on the wall with all the neighbours looking down at them, and Maisie holding them tightly, while men wearing white coats took their father away in an ambulance. Terry was inside with Gladys. Gladys came out looking very sad and upset, and, covering her head, told the neighbours, "Get away from the house! The show is over; have some respect." Gladys then told Teresa and Tabitha, "You two go to Maisie's for tea and she will bring you home later". The girls were full of questions, but no answers were being given, so they were very upset. They couldn't eat the food, both saying they weren't hungry. Tabitha was feeling unwell and later threw up. She was in shock from seeing all the activity with police and doctors at her house. Teresa heard Maisie say to Dan, "Aged eleven and eight. They are still children, trying to make sense of everything". Pamela couldn't believe that the girls weren't allowed in their own house, and didn't really understand why Teresa's dad would beat her. Finally, Dan and Maisie put Teresa, Tabitha and their daughter Pamela into the car to take them home.

On entering the house, Teresa could smell polish and bleach. She saw that the furniture in the dining room was broken to pieces, as were the pictures on the wall. She also noticed blood on the wall and the stairs and wondered whose blood it was this time. Then, Gladys appeared, her arm in a sling and with a massive bandage put around the large cut on her head. Dan and Maisie were talking to Gladys, and Maisie said she was staying, and Dan was to take Pamela back home. Terry came out of his room to see Teresa and Tabitha and told them that their dad had gone mad and had to go to a special hospital. The police had made him go. "How do you know?" Teresa asked Terry replied, "I came home and saw them talking to Dad, telling him he had to go, while the doctors were seeing to Mum". Terry went on to say, "I helped Mum get the place right before you came home". Teresa replied,

"Why is there blood on the wallpaper and on the wall?" "Oh, I must have missed some; I had to pull some wallpaper off as Mum didn't want blood showing on it." Gladys called the girls into the room, saying, "Your father isn't well. He had to go to hospital to make him better. You will see him, though, as we will be visiting him all the time. But right now, we must carry on as normal." With that, she then checked over Teresa's body since he had pushed her down the stairs. She turned to Maisie and said, "Look at this! How could he do this to her?" Teresa, feeling brave, said, "Don't worry, I'm okay." Maisie said to Teresa, "Are you sure you're okay? Are you sure? You must be sore." "No," replied Teresa.

Hours later, after watching TV, the children went to bed. Gladys and Maisie sat talking downstairs. Terry went into Teresa's room and said, "Don't worry, sis, he won't hurt you again." Teresa replied, "You said that last time". Tabitha asked Teresa, "Is he going to hit me like he hits you and Terry? "No," Teresa said, "I promise you." Both Terry and Teresa were lying awake, unable to sleep that night when they heard the doorbell ring. They looked out and it was Nana Jane, standing there in the pouring rain with her umbrella. Gladys answered the door, then Nana Jane grabbed Gladys's hair. They were fighting in the hallway. Nana shouted, "What have you done with my son? You're a trollop!" Gladys replied, "Me? That's a laugh, with your history! Pot calling the kettle black." Maisie quickly intervened, trying to calm the situation, but Gladys pushed Jane out of the house and she fell on the wet floor outside. It was then she noticed Uncle Ben was waiting in the car. Nana Jane, soaking wet, walked back to the car, shouting abuse at Gladys; "Bitch! Whore!" then Gladys shouted, "Where's your other kids, Jane? Get away from here; you've caused all of this." Unbeknown to Gladys, Terry and Teresa had watched it all and found it funny when Nana Jane fell on the floor outside. Did she fall or was she pushed? Either way, the children found it funny; that was the first time they had laughed all day. Terry and Teresa both went back to bed. Tabitha slept through it, oblivious to it all.

Maisie stayed with Gladys all night, and the children had the rest of that week off school. The following morning, Terry said to Gladys, "Are we going to see Dad?" Gladys replied, "Not today. He needs time to settle in and I want to talk to you all." When all the children came down, Gladys sat down beside them and started to explain. She told them as plainly as she could that their father had suffered what was called a nervous breakdown, and needed special treatment. She went on to say that he could be in hospital for months. Teresa then asked, "Why were the police here?" "I called them," she replied. "He was out of control. He wouldn't listen to me, so I left the house whilst he was in the bathroom, called the Doctor, and he then told me I had to call the police." Terry then said, "I don't want him to come back; he hurt me," "Neither do I," said Tabitha. Teresa replied, "Mum just said he's ill. He's had a nervous breakdown, but what is that?" Gladys explained "It's to do with the brain in your head; it's not working properly. That's why your father gets nervous and angry." Still not taking it all in, or understanding, the children carried on as usual.

Weeks passed and their father was still in hospital. Teresa went the most often to see her father as he always needed to see her for some reason, and she was good company for her mother Gladys. On the way back from hospital one day, Teresa was carrying a table lamp her father had made for her in hospital. She was very talkative, saying "I want Dad home; do you think he can come home?" Gladys replied, "No, not yet." "Why not?" asked Teresa. "He must be getting better, making lamps and being kind to us." "He can't come home yet; he's telling lies to the doctors. Why do you think I was talking to the doctors for such a long time?" She went on to say, "He told the doctors I spent all his money and gave him a bad life. Oh, and I'm nasty to Nana Jane." Teresa then said, "Has Dad got brothers or sisters?" "What do you mean?" asked Gladys. "The night she came around, you asked her where her other kids were. Me and Terry heard you." Gladys went on to say, "Your Nana came from another town when your dad was a baby. She took a job as a housekeeper for Uncle Ben, leaving her husband and five children behind; she only took your father. At the time, Uncle Ben was seeing a nurse, but he stopped seeing her when Nana Jane moved into the house with your father." "Does she see her children, then?" Teresa asked. Gladys replied, "Yes, but they're all grown up now and live in different towns with children of their own. Your cousins." "Oh," replied Teresa.

Teresa thought a lot about her cousins as she never knew she had any. Teresa, being curious, asked, "Why haven't I seen them?" Gladys replied, "Because they live far away and only visit Nana Jane."

Chapter 7

Strangers Come to the House

When they reached home, Maisie and Pamela were at the house; they had stayed to look after Terry and Tabitha. Teresa called Terry, Tabitha, and Pamela to go outside where she told them the secret of the cousins. Terry replied, "Well, I've never seen them at Nana Jane's, so maybe they don't like Nana Jane?" Teresa said, "No way!" Terry replied. With that, Teresa showed them the lamp Michael had made. Terry hated it and Tabitha said nothing. Another few weeks passed, and Michael was being discharged after his last ECT treatment. Deep down, Gladys wanted to know why Michael had lied to the doctors, but she didn't want an argument and thought if he took his medication, things should be better.

The day had come, and Michael was discharged and told not to work for a couple more weeks. Gladys couldn't wait for Michael to return to work as money was tighter than ever, and him coming home would be a test to see if he was better, especially around the children. Gladys laid down the law to Michael, saying, "You can come home on one condition; that Nana Jane doesn't come to the house ever again". Michael agreed. The children weren't sure if they wanted their father home. Terry definitely didn't, Teresa wasn't sure, and neither was Tabitha. When Michael walked into the house, Tabitha had the giggles, a nervous giggle. Terry looked at him and immediately went to his room. Teresa put the kettle on and gave her mother and father tea and biscuits. "You're a good girl," Michael said to Teresa. "And I am sorry; you know that, right?" Teresa replied, "Yes." Tabitha sat by Gladys, not knowing what to think, but was talking to her father. Terry ignored him, causing an atmosphere. It was clear there was a massive divide in the family. "Terry was always Mum's favourite," thought Teresa. "That's why he hasn't been told off. He thinks he's big, but he's just a bighead."

The house had been redecorated since the incident and was looking nice. There was new red rose wallpaper on the walls up the stairs, and the fresh smell of paint, but the new furniture was still broken, and Teresa still didn't have a radio. Later that day, Maisie and Dan came to see Michael, and Michael thanked them for the support they had given his family during his absence in hospital. Maisie and Dan had decided to buy Teresa her new uniform as they knew Gladys was struggling with money. Both Teresa and Pamela were going to the big school, the comprehensive girls-only school, after the holidays. Maisie and Dan were true friends and Gladys always said, "You know your friends when the chips are down". And as far as Nana Jane was concerned, the hospital staff had told Gladys that she didn't even inquire how her son was during his stay in hospital, but she wasn't at all surprised.

The school term resumed with Terry off to the boys' comprehensive, and Teresa off to the girls' comprehensive. But Tabitha was very reluctant to go back to her junior school. In fact, Gladys walked with her for a while as she was too nervous to go without her big sister Teresa. The children were only back to school a few days when she had a letter from Michael's sister Myfanwy and her husband Robert. They stated in the letter that they were disgusted with Nana Jane's actions and asked if they could visit. Myfanwy was very worried about her brother. They had put their phone number on the letter for Gladys to ring them if she so wished. After careful thought, Gladys agreed. She rang them and spoke for a short time as Gladys was in a phone box, and arrangements were made for the following Saturday afternoon. Michael was elated that his sister was coming as she had never seen his children and it had been a long time since he had seen her. The children were told best clothes, best behaviour. They also noticed that Gladys had bought fruit for the table, and foods the children had never had, or seen before; the pantry was full. Saturday arrived; the children waited at the window. Gladys was dressed up with her make-up on and wearing her high heels. Tensions grew as they waited, and Michael and Gladys both sat in the best room with tea and cigarettes. A black shiny Jaguar car pulled up outside, and three people got out, all dressed very smartly with posh hats on, and walked down the garden path to the house. Tabitha ran into the best room to tell her mother and father they were there. Michael headed to the door to greet them. Gladys went to the kitchen to make tea and coffee, and the bone china cups and saucers from the cabinet came out, as did the teapot. Gladys then told Teresa to put a selection of biscuits on a tea plate, which she did. Terry came into the kitchen, saw the biscuits and asked, "Can I have one?" "No!" shouted Gladys. She then called Tabitha into the kitchen and said to all three children, "All this food is for the visitors, as we will be having a special tea tonight. So, when I ask you if you want any more, you must say, "No, Mum, thank you." Teresa looked at Terry who was loving the look of all this nice food. Then Terry said, "Why should they have it? It's our food". Gladys told him to Shush and behave himself. But all three children thought that wasn't fair. Gladys took her nice tray into the room for guests only; nothing for the children. Terry said to Teresa, "Are you thirsty?" Tabitha then shouted, "Yes!" Teresa asked, "Why?" "Mum's got pop in the pantry." "Pop?" said Teresa. "Yes," replied Terry. "Grab a cup!" They each got a cup and Terry filled them with pop. There were all different flavours, just like at Nana Jane's House. All three children were in the pantry with the door shut, drinking the forbidden pop and chuckling.

Gladys came out of the room and called all three children into the best room to meet their visitors, but Teresa and Tabitha had red pop all over their mouths, so they quickly ran to the bathroom to rub it off. Gladys knew what they had done, but they were told to wait until the visitors had gone and she would sort them out then. The girls knew they were in trouble, but not Terry, of course. Teresa gave him a dirty look, but Terry sniggered, and said to Teresa, "You shouldn't have chosen red, should you?" The children entered the room and were introduced to Michael's sister Myfanwy and her husband Robert, along with Michael's other sister, Winnie. Gladys then introduced them all; "This is Terry; he's growing into a fine young man. This is Teresa; she will make someone a good wife someday. And this is Tabitha; she's the youngest". Teresa said, "Wife?" and Gladys said, "Yes, because you are a great help around the house." With that, she asked Teresa to take the tray out, relay it, and bring a fresh pot of tea in, but Robert said, "Not for me, Gladys. If I can, could I have coffee?" "Coffee?" replied Gladys. "Of course! I will help Teresa, as she makes awful coffee." Teresa thought, "Why would she say that? We never have coffee in the house". Gladys got up and followed Teresa into the kitchen saying, "Good girl for not saying anything.

Don't want them thinking we don't stock coffee." "What are you all talking about in the room?" Teresa asked. Gladys replied, "Nothing to concern you, it's just about your father, and after this, I will be out to lay the table for tea. And don't forget what I told you about more food. If there's anything left, you three can have it." Gladys then took the tray back into the room, sending Terry and Tabitha out.

The three children decided to go out and were told not to get dirty or go too far as their tea wouldn't be long. Outside they went and spotted Robert's car; it really looked out of place outside a council house. Terry said to Teresa and Tabitha, "I like the car. I'm going to have a sports car one day". "Me too," said Teresa. "I'll have a white one." Terry replied, "No, you won't, you're a girl; you'll be married one day, and your husband will have one if he's rich." "I will have one," replied Teresa, then Tabitha said to Terry, "Won't you crash?" Terry replied, "No, only Teresa will crash because she's a girl!" Tabitha then said, "Please don't get a car, Teresa. I will miss you." "Take no notice of bighead there; he's full of shit," said Teresa, using language she had learned from her father. Terry then chased Teresa, who ran straight in through the back door, nearly colliding with the visitors who were all helping to lay the table. "Sorry," she said as Terry stood behind her laughing. Teresa gave him a threatening look. All three children were told by Gladys to put the TV on in the best room, and she would call them when tea was ready.

They had only been in the room for five minutes when Robert, or Uncle Robert to them, walked in. He sat down with them and told them about where he lived. "I have a large house which is nearly opposite the beach; you only have to turn one corner and you're there," he said. Teresa asked, "Have you got children?" "Yes," he replied. "I have two sons; they are older than you. They both work, and are both in their twenties. I'm sure you will like them when you meet them." "Are we going to meet them?" asked Teresa. "Yes, I'm sure you are going to one day. So, you love the beach, do you, Teresa? Your father says you do." "I love the beach! It's fun and all the people on the beach look tiny when you're in the water," she replied. He then went on to say, "Maybe one day, you can all come and stay. Would you like that?" Teresa and Tabitha replied, "Yes!" "What about you, Terry? Would you like that?" Terry quietly replied, "Yes".

Terry didn't know what to make of them; any of them. He remained quiet for the duration of the visit. Gladys called the children into the dining room, and they sat at the table. Teresa sat opposite Robert; she liked him. He was kind and kept smiling and winking at her. None of the children knew what to do with food like this, and they had never had anything so posh! There was salad, dainty sandwiches, cake, salmon, and a selection of different cheeses, crackers, and drinks galore. Terry couldn't wait for them to go as he wanted things the visitors were eating and feared there would be nothing left. Then, as they had been told, Gladys asked the children, "Would you like anymore?" They all replied, "No, thank you, Mum". Winnie then said, "What lovely children you are and so polite". Winnie was eating cake with a fork; "Who does that?" Teresa thought. Michael, smiling at his children, said, "Yes, they're not too bad".

All three children got down from the table and went into the room to watch TV, whilst all the visitors, Michael, and Gladys cleared away and washed the dishes. They stayed in the dining room for another hour talking to Michael and Gladys. The children didn't go into the dining room as they were watching TV later than usual and thought they must have a lot to talk about. Suddenly, Gladys called the children to say goodbye. The visitors put their posh hats and coats on and said goodbye to the children individually. Winnie went first saying goodbye, then next, Myfanwy, who gave them all a big hug. Then Robert, who shook their hands, giving them each half a crown and saying "Don't tell your mother." Even Terry liked him then. Teresa then noticed Robert putting a roll of pound notes into Gladys's hands and closing her hand for no one to see. Michael was smiling, escorting them out, and stood at their car, talking yet again. Teresa wondered what else they could be talking about. Gladys turned to the children and said, "If you're still hungry, go to the pantry. There are sandwiches and other food which must be eaten today." Terry was first there, then Tabitha, whilst Teresa asked her mum, "How much money did Uncle Robert give you?" "What money?" replied Gladys. "I saw," said Teresa. "He gave us half a crown each; all of us." "Did he now?" said Gladys. "Yes, he's a kind man; I like Uncle Robert," said Teresa. "Uncle Robert did give me some money as you saw, Teresa, but you mustn't tell your father; it's not a lot," she said. Teresa replied, "Okay". Michael came into the room and said to Gladys, "The day went well, don't you think?" "Yes, it did. Everyone appeared to enjoy themselves and the children really liked them. Robert gave them all half a crown." "Really?" replied Michael. "I know Robert was asking about Teresa, and she told him she liked the beach. I can't remember the last time I had a conversation with her, or the others, come to that. I really don't know my children, do I?" Gladys replied, "I think we are both guilty of that, what with the life they've had. No wonder Tabitha is nervous of everything; she relies on Teresa more than me. Terry isn't progressing that well at school. He's doing okay, but nothing special, and Teresa, I find, is strong-willed and her own person who never shows us her true feelings. She appears the least affected by the situation, but we've got to change." In a way, Michael was hurt, as he knew his children were suffering, and deep down, knew it was his fault. Teresa did appear to be the strongest, but was she really? "Why do I hurt my own children?" he asked himself.

PART II

Chapter 1

Changes

The years progressed and the children were slowly becoming young adults. Regarding the changes, the family saw their relations quite often, and as promised, stayed a week at Uncle Robert's house for a holiday. There they met their cousins, Anthony and Raymond, who were very kind, and they went on walks with their newly found relations to get to know each other. Uncle Robert's house was big, just like he said, and he and Myfanwy ran a bed and breakfast there. Not only was the beach just around the corner, but there were also lots of other sites in the surrounding area. Teresa remembered going into a park, a huge park with a big mansion-type house. She then called to Gladys saying, "Look, Mum! I've been here before". Gladys replied, "No, Teresa, you haven't." "I have," said Teresa, "I can show you where the kitchen is." Gladys then agreed to go with Teresa for her to show her the kitchen. To her surprise, Teresa was right, and the kitchen was where she said. Gladys was puzzled as she knew Teresa hadn't been brought here before, not even on a school trip. Gladys had no explanation, but just said to Teresa, "Yes, you are right. I really don't know how you know."

After the park visit, Uncle Robert took the family to see the witches. He drove up a very steep, winding hill, going around and around, and there they were - the witches - lit up in lights. Teresa loved this but Tabitha loved it more, and, to top it off, there was a café at the top shaped like an apple. All the family enjoyed their day, and enjoyed every day thereafter, being taken to different tourist attractions and truly spoilt during the week. And as for Teresa, it was something she would never forget as the week felt like magic. Sadly, there were no more holidays for the children after that, just several moves as Gladys was working her way back down to the bottom of the estate, near her first house, where Teresa had been born. This was to be the final move, she would promise each time they moved. Uncle Robert would be staying as usual. He visited mostly on his own as his work would bring him to the town, and he would always decorate the new houses whilst Michael was at work. Terry started a paper round to earn money, and Teresa used to work on the pop van and the bread van, so she could also earn money during the school holidays.

Those holidays always went very fast, and before they knew it, they were back in school. One morning, before going to school, Teresa ventured into her mother's bedroom for a hair clip, when she discovered something nasty-looking on the floor beside the bed. Curiosity was getting the better of her. She went up to it to investigate. "What's this?" she thought. "I've never seen anything like this before." She rushed to the bathroom for some tissue, and picked the object up. As she walked downstairs, her mother was in the hallway. Teresa asked her, "What's this, Mum?" Gladys turned as red as a beetroot, and, looking really embarrassed, said to Teresa, "Give it here now; it's not for you to know." Teresa was puzzled, and as she was leaving for school, Gladys called her and said, "I don't know what you think you found, but you mustn't tell your father because he will get embarrassed, and we don't want rows and fights, do we?" That was the last thing Teresa wanted, as Gladys and Michael still rowed a lot, but the violence appeared to have calmed down lately. Teresa started to think to herself that Gladys had told her not to tell her father a lot of things over the years. She never told anyone, and always kept her mother's secrets, as she now decided they were. If not secrets, why couldn't she tell her father? She thought about it and then carried on with her schoolwork.

Her mother had never talked to Teresa about the facts of life. She hadn't even told her what periods were for girls; she had to find out from a teacher in school one day when they started. In fact, life conversations never really happened between siblings and parents. The following weekend, a huge argument broke out between Gladys and Michael. It was over a letter that had arrived, and it was something to do with Auntie Myfanwy. Gladys shouted out loud, "How dare she say such things!" and Michael replied, "Why would she say a thing like that, then?" Gladys ended the discussion by saying to Michael, "Think what you like, Michael". Michael went to see

Nana Jane. Teresa did not understand any of it. But Terry said, "I know what it's about. Haven't you noticed Mum and Uncle Robert always sitting close together in the room and holding hands?" Teresa replied, "No, they don't!" "Yes, they do," Terry said. "Remember, you were very ill with spots on your face one day and Mum still made you go to school?" "Yes," Teresa replied. "Uncle Robert came and fetched me with Mum when school called her." "Yes, they did," replied Terry. "There's something going on with them." "What do you mean?" Teresa asked Terry. Terry was nearly fifteen now, and due to leave school soon. He said, "They are having an affair." Teresa knew what that was, as her friends and her always spoke of boys, love, and affairs in school, and one girl, who was only fifteen years old, was expelled from school because she was having a baby. Teresa was learning about life but was still quite naïve.

Over the coming weeks, Uncle Robert still visited, but this time, Teresa was watching for the behaviour that Terry had pointed out to her. He was still staying overnight as usual when he worked in town, but Teresa didn't believe Terry. "He must be wrong," she thought. "Dad wouldn't let him stay, would he?" Teresa was convinced there was nothing to it as Tabitha stayed in the most and was always around Mum and Uncle Robert. Since then, there had been an uneasy atmosphere between Michael and Uncle Robert, but they soon returned to normal, especially when the children were around. When he was at home, Michael spent a lot of time in the garden where he grew rows and rows of vegetables and made Terry help him. Terry hated it as he had no interest at all, and there didn't appear to be any father-son bond between them. They argued regularly, but one day, Terry decided it would be a good idea to put empty tins of baked beans and peas upside down in rows in his garden. Terry saved all the tins he could, then, one day, he said, "Hey, Dad, your vegetables have grown really big," and he shot upstairs. Michael went out of the back door and saw what Terry had done. He was ballistic, throwing the empty cans off his vegetable garden. He then charged into the kitchen, almost knocking Teresa and Tabitha over, as they were making tea for the family. Michael ran upstairs, and shouted at Terry, "You think that was funny, do you? Do you?!" He started thumping Terry, but Terry hit back. He was fifteen years old now and about to leave school, so he wasn't going to just stand there and take it. Gladys intervened and tried to protect Terry, and stop Michael. But she couldn't. Terry ran downstairs and out of the front door. A furious Michael blamed Gladys for not teaching him respect. "Respect?" retorted Gladys. "Respect is earned, not just given." "That's right," replied Michael. "You always take his side." Michael walked into the kitchen, and said to Teresa and Tabitha, "You know he's the favourite, don't you? He will never be made to help around the house. I feel sorry for you two little skivvies, whilst both your mother and your brother are living the high life." Teresa and Tabitha look on whilst Gladys replied, "Oh, don't you feel sorry for yourself, will you, Michael?" Michael gave no answer and went back to tending his garden and vegetables.

Tabitha said to Teresa, "I think Daddy's right, because every day I have off school, we are always cleaning. I can't see my friends because of you; I've got to help you." Teresa replied, "Yes, you do because I must make sure all the washing and ironing is done on the weekend." Teresa thought Tabitha must be noticing a lot now to say that, so she asked her about Robert. "What do you like about Uncle Robert?" "I don't like him," Tabitha replied. She went on to explain; "When he is here, they always whisper in front of me so I won't hear things. I feel in the way," she said. Teresa asked, "Has Mum ever told you not to tell Dad anything?" "No," said Tabitha. "Why?" "Oh, never mind then, I just wondered," said Teresa. Tabitha said, "I can't wait for the end of term, as I will be going to the girl's school with you, won't I?" "Yes, you will," Teresa replied.

Over the coming weeks, the girls decided that one day, they would go out and see their friends, thinking why should they do all the work while Terry was out with his mates? This they did, but Gladys came out after them and told them they could go out to see their friends after the work was done. Teresa retaliated and said, "No. We want to stay out. It isn't fair. Terry's out." Gladys ignored that last remark and made the girls go back into the house. The twin tub was pulled out ready for Teresa to start the washing. There were piles of it on the floor, but Tabitha went straight upstairs, refusing to help with the chores. Gladys told Teresa to carry on, otherwise, the washing wouldn't dry today, and as for Tabitha, she said, "She's not as old as you".

Teresa turned to Gladys and said in a temper, "Why don't you do it? I always do it. Dad is right about you!" Gladys replied, "Your father is right about nothing; just do as you are told or look out as my patience is now running thin." Teresa carried on, and when she was hanging the washing on the line, Tabitha was at the bedroom window, smiling. Teresa felt used and abused as Tabitha never got into trouble. And there was Terry with his teenage friends walking around doing nothing. Teresa was packing away the twin tub washing machine when she heard Gladys shouting, "Teresa, make a cup of tea, please, when you've finished?" Teresa took her time just to be awkward but eventually, she made her mother a cup of tea. Teresa had just gone upstairs and got changed to hang out with her friends, when her mother shouted again, "Teresa, can you make us a cup of tea as Uncle Robert has arrived?" "You've just had one," Teresa said. Gladys replied, "I told you, Uncle Robert has arrived." "He drinks coffee," replied Teresa. "Just do as you're told," said Gladys. Teresa was furious and stormed downstairs to the kitchen. She made her mother a cup of tea and coffee for Uncle Robert. She then took the tray to the sitting room and handed Uncle Robert his coffee. She put the tray down and handed her mother her tea, but her hand slipped, and she dropped the cup. Gladys jumped, shouting and screaming, as boiling hot tea had landed in her lap. Uncle Robert quickly put his hands up her skirt to remove her girdle, forgetting that Teresa was present. Her uncle then realised his mistake, and Gladys carried on removing the wet underwear saying to Teresa, "You did this on purpose! You are a horrible, horrible girl. Get out of my sight." Teresa walked out of the room apologising, then walked straight out of the front door to be with her friends. Her thoughts were running riot. "How did he know Mum wore a girdle? You just don't put your hands up anyone's skirt, do you? Or maybe in an emergency, you do?" Teresa didn't know. Only one thing was certain - it was an accident. It wasn't done on purpose, but later, she laughed at the image of her mother jumping around. When Teresa came back into the house that evening, Uncle Robert gave her a dirty look, as if telling her he was ashamed to see what she had done. But Teresa didn't care. He wasn't her father. He couldn't do anything. Terry returned home, so Teresa told him what had happened. He replied, "Just go out, Teresa. You do everything. Don't do the chores anymore, because I won't," he said. "And Tabitha doesn't really have to anyway." Teresa knew he was right; after all, she thought, "Mum doesn't do a lot. What does she do when we're in school? And it isn't as if she works."

Over the weeks that followed, Teresa did her chores, but not all. Gladys noticed this and asked her why half the work wasn't done. Teresa replied, "I shouldn't have to do it; it's not fair. Do it yourself instead of just sitting on the settee." Gladys slapped Teresa in the face and told her, "You are an ungrateful Madam and you can say goodbye to the new clothes you wanted." Teresa was very upset; she wanted some boots and midi skirts out of the catalogue; she went to her room crying. Michael was becoming very aware of the tensions between mother and daughter, so tried talking to Teresa, telling her that she should do as her mother tells her and that he would tell Gladys to order the clothes. Michael did just that when another row broke out, with Gladys saying no but Michael saying yes. Teresa overheard him say, "She does a lot for you and you don't appreciate her, or myself, come to that; it's just Terry, the perfect son." Gladys told him to get out. Doors slammed then all went quiet. Teresa was sitting, chin in her hands, thinking, "Why me all the time? I never see the others work as hard around the house, including Mother." And of course, that was exactly how things were in the household, but in those days, it was always the females who did the cooking and cleaning, as this was considered good education for when they got married. Women were considered to have little or no rights during these years. But times were changing; women were now having a voice. They were standing up for themselves and future generations, though not fast enough for Teresa. Her generation were just called troublemakers, as protests for women's rights and gender equality were really on the rise during the sixties and seventies.

Chapter 2

Possible Opportunities

Months flew by. Michael didn't leave; as he told Gladys, he paid the rent. Tabitha joined Teresa at the big school, as she was now eleven. As Tabitha was starting, Terry was leaving, and had taken up a good opportunity in the motor industry; he was offered an apprenticeship in a local garage. Terry was made up, and full of ideas for his future. Teresa was in the last year of her school and started noticing boys, especially one. This boy was older and not in school, and he used to drive around the estate in his lovely black Ford Cortina car. He always had the top down so Teresa thought it looked like a sports car. Each evening, Teresa would walk around to the shops with her friends, and he would beep his horn and make them all laugh. Elizabeth, Teresa's friend, stopped his car by putting her hand up. The car stopped, and this handsome boy said, "What's your names?" "Teresa," she replied. Elizabeth then introduced herself. He smiled at them both and said, "Jump in the car!" The girls looked at each other and, without a care or any hesitation, they jumped in. He took Elizabeth and Teresa for a ride, out from the estate, and up to the mountain nearby, their hair blowing in the wind and feeling quite cold, but refreshing and free. Teresa spread her arms out wide, and, laughing out loud, she could not hide her joy; they were having great fun. Teresa asked, "What's your name and where do you live?" "My name is David," he replied, "David Kennedy, and I live up on top of the mountain." He was a farmer's son, "and a spoilt one at that," she thought. Teresa wanted to know more about David. She was a love-struck teenager, and he had a car; she couldn't stop smiling. A couple of times, David took Elizabeth and Teresa for a ride in his car, but he liked Teresa, and Teresa liked him.

One time, David asked Teresa if he could pick her up from school the following day. Teresa agreed but had to say, "My sister and Elizabeth will be with me too, as we walk home together." Teresa told Tabitha that evening but told her not to tell their parents. She went on informing Tabitha of how handsome he was, better than younger boys or boys the same age. She was smitten and excited. The next morning, Teresa and Tabitha walked to school with their friends. Teresa had a skip in her step and Elizabeth wanted to know everything. At the last corner before school, the children would always watch for the headmistress, Mrs Bowden, as she would make one of the children, whoever was passing, carry her briefcase and bags to her office. They waited as she pulled up in her Morris Minor car. Mrs Bowden then asked one of the other girls. So, Teresa and her friends walked down the hill and in through the school gates. Lessons that day went too slow for Teresa. Finally, the school bell rang and the teacher said, "All rise; pack your books away, and have a safe journey home." Teresa rushed down the long corridors to Tabitha's classroom, fetched her coat for her, and ran outside. There he was, David Kennedy, in his shiny black car. "Is that him?" Tabitha asked. "Yes," Teresa replied, holding Tabitha's hand, and in the car they got. Tabitha and Elizabeth sat in the back and Teresa in the front.

David drove the car quite fast and pulled up outside their house. Tabitha and Elizabeth got out but Teresa stayed in as she and David were talking. Tabitha told Gladys because she had spotted the car and was watching behind the curtain. Half an hour passed then there was a knock on the car window. It was Gladys, telling Teresa to come inside. A few minutes later, Teresa went inside to face all the questions that she knew would be asked. Gladys knew he was older as he drove a car. "You're too young to be thinking about boys, and you know what boys want!" "We just talk," replied Teresa. For the rest of the week, David picked up Teresa, Elizabeth and Tabitha from school. Then he asked Teresa if he could see her on Saturday evening. Teresa was so happy; she was in love with the handsome David Kennedy, and they had kissed. Teresa met up with her friend Elizabeth and told her everything. Elizabeth was worried for her friend and warned her what boys were like and told her to be careful as a boy had tried it on with her.

Saturday came, and Teresa put on her lovely high boots and midi skirt, white blouse, jewellery, and a small amount of makeup, but no lipstick. Michael smiled when he saw Teresa, saying, "You look beautiful, my girl. Have a nice time, but remember back home before eight-thirty". Gladys, however, was not very pleased as she thought Teresa was too young and emphasised the 'be in on time' rule. David and Teresa drove around the estate, talking to friends, before David pulled into a layby. They kissed and talked. The time was approaching seven-thirty, so Teresa only had another hour before going in. David started trying it on and became very passionate, so when Teresa rejected his passes, he said, "Well, when?" Teresa said, "Maybe in the future". David respected Teresa's wishes and took her home. David needed to pass Teresa's house to get home, so, when he stayed out later, Teresa would sit on the wall until he passed, as he would stop and talk to her. David carried on meeting Teresa at school to take her, Elizabeth and her sister home. The weekend came again and it was just the same as last week. Teresa would go out with David but rejected his passes. She was afraid she would become pregnant like the girl who got expelled; she was only fifteen. David was getting fed up with waiting and he told Teresa, "I've waited and been more than patient. I don't think you ever will, Teresa". "I just can't," she said. "I don't know why as I do love you back." David started the car and said very little after that, and took Teresa home a little earlier, not even kissing her goodnight. Teresa ran into her house crying. She sobbed into her pillow, not understanding why he needed to do that. Later that evening, she went to her gate to see him before he went home, but as he passed, he looked at her and drove straight on without stopping. Teresa was now waiting for Monday in the hope that he would pick her up from school.

Monday morning came and Teresa confided in Elizabeth, asking her what she would do as she didn't want to lose David. Elizabeth told her to do nothing; if he loved her back, he would wait. Monday morning came, and off to school the girls went. Teresa was still thinking of David as she couldn't think of anything else. Then, during assembly, Mrs Bowden called out her name and asked her to come onto the stage. A few other girls were also called. Teresa's mind was in overdrive, as you're usually only called if you've done something wrong. Teresa knew a few of her friends had put a condom behind the radiator in the staff room, but she wasn't involved with that. Teresa started to worry as Mrs Bowden was very strict and frightening. Mrs Bowden then faced the other children and said, "These girls have achieved good grades by working hard, and are a good example for this girl's school, so, for this, we all decided in a staff meeting that these are to be the new prefects." Teresa felt a sigh of relief, as did Tabitha, as she thought her sister was in big trouble, being called to the stage. Teresa was congratulated by Mrs Bowden, who shook her hand, whilst giving her a prefect badge. It was a great honour if you were a prefect; it meant you had a prefect's room and would help teachers when needed. You would line the corridors as pupils came in making sure they stayed in line and didn't run. With this badge came responsibilities, but also, you got to stay in at break times. Brilliant for the cold and rainy days! Teresa was elated, as were her friends, as nobody picked on a prefect; they wouldn't dare. If the pupils were caught doing anything wrong, a prefect could keep them in at break time and give them lines. And, of course, they could inform the teachers. Teresa couldn't wait for the bell to go that day as she wanted to tell David her news. But when the school day ended, David wasn't there to pick her up. Teresa waited until all the children had left but still no David. Tabitha went on walking home with Elizabeth, but Teresa was holding back her tears while slowly walking home alone, hoping all the way that David would pull up alongside her. Meanwhile, Tabitha had already told Gladys and Michael Teresa's news, but a very upset Teresa couldn't care less. Later that evening, Teresa went out with a few of her friends and best friend Elizabeth. David was nowhere to be seen. He always drove around the shops at night. Where was he, Teresa wondered? That night, Teresa waited on the wall until ten pm but then she had to go in as her mother told her not to be so silly. As she was closing the front gate, David drove by, but he never stopped. Teresa was heartbroken; she cried herself to sleep that night knowing David didn't want to bother with her anymore. He was her first love, the handsome David with his car. Days passed, but Teresa never saw him at all as he wasn't hanging out around the shops on the estate anymore.

However, with the help of Elizabeth, Teresa got over him quite quickly. She was now enjoying spending time with her girlfriends and had also got herself a Saturday job in a supermarket in town, which was good money, good being better than no money. A few days later as she came out of school, Elizabeth spotted David and told Teresa, and as they were walking out of the school gates, they saw Jennifer Jacobs get into David's car. They were both shocked as they watched them drive off. "Jennifer bloody Jacobs," said Teresa. "No wonder we haven't seen them because she lives in the next village." Elizabeth then said, "She does things with boys, so that's why." Jennifer Jacobs had long blonde hair, and the most massive tits anyone had ever seen. She had a bad name, which explained a lot. Jennifer was in the year below Teresa, and she was so gobby. From then on, Teresa would pull her out and make her do lines. Being a prefect came in handy. She should have made her write "'I will not steal anybody's boyfriend again", but Teresa couldn't make her write that, so instead, she made her write, "I will not talk in line anymore". Teresa had certainly learned one lesson - he just wanted one thing. And as for Jennifer, she gave it, and he moved on; she also knew Jennifer wouldn't be crying over him.

Time flew by once again and Christmas had passed. Teresa was enjoying her Saturday job and doing well at school. Terry, however, was enjoying his apprenticeship but was throwing his weight around the house. Michael felt he should be paying board and lodging, but Gladys would tell Michael, "Leave him alone. He doesn't earn a lot on an apprenticeship." Terry would give Michael a noticeable smirk, which infuriated Michael. No love lost there; they really disliked each other. Tabitha was growing in confidence, and now had plenty of friends. She used to invite them home and they would stay overnight on occasions. Uncle Robert, however, was still staying regularly whilst working in the town, and he arranged for a telephone to be connected to the house. This Gladys loved, while Michael only thought of the bills, and whose house was it anyway? All the family enjoyed the phone, but they were on a party line, as the post office called it. This meant that they shared with other people, so no call was private if the other people lifted their receiver. Uncle Robert called the post office many times for them to be put on a private line and eventually, they were. Michael was happy for him to do this as he wanted nothing to do with it. It wasn't his idea to have a telephone installed, so, tensions were still very high in the house. Nobody really spoke to each other at all. Michael chose to go into the back room some evenings when he felt he didn't want to talk to anyone. The room consisted of a two-seater settee, one armchair, one coffee table, and one lamp. He would get up in the morning, make his toast and boiled egg, and, with newspaper in hand, take it to his room. Gladys would say to the children, "Don't go into the room; he's obviously got it on him again. Stay out from there".

One Friday evening, at approximately five-thirty, a knock came at the door; it was Mrs Bowden, the headmistress of the girl's school. Gladys answered the door and invited her into the front room whilst going to the back room to fetch Michael. Mrs Bowden said she was there to discuss Teresa, so, Tabitha and Terry were sent out of the room. Mrs Bowden asked, "Why have you not replied to my letters?" Gladys replied, "I didn't think they were important". Michael asked, "What letters?" Mrs Bowden went on to say, "Three letters have been sent inviting you to school to discuss Teresa's progress." Michael knew nothing; he wasn't happy that Gladys hadn't told him anything about the letters. Mrs Bowden then went on to say that Teresa was extremely good at maths and English, and in her opinion, it would be in Teresa's best interest for her to go to college, as she believed Teresa could have a great future. "She's a very clever girl, you know." Teresa's eyes lit up. "Although I'm good at English and maths," she thought, "I'm rubbish at history, geography etc." However, she thought it would be great, and she could get one up on her brother. Teresa was excited, as was Michael, as he was very clever in school, so much so that they had to keep him home from school for a year for others to catch up; he was very advanced. Gladys said to Mrs Bowden, "It is very irregular for girls to go to college. I think it's more important for boys, and Teresa has already got a job, and will most probably get married and have children, therefore, she won't be going to any college." She went on to say, "It would just be a waste". Mrs Bowden got up to leave and said to Michael and Gladys, "Please think hard about this; girls should be given the same opportunities as boys, and please talk to your daughter Teresa, then let me know your final decision. I will leave it with you," she said, as she left the house.

After Mrs Bowden had left, the conversation erupted as Michael was very angry, saying to Gladys, "There was a discussion about Terry and his future, but when it comes to Teresa, you just don't care, do you?" He was leaning his face right in front of Gladys's. "Correspondence from the school was meant for me, not only you!" he yelled. "What gives you the right to hide letters concerning my children?" Gladys told him, "Calm down and go back to your den, as she's not going, and that's final. We can't afford it." Michael retaliated and said, "It's not for you to decide. It's Teresa's decision and depends on how she feels about it. And as for affording it, you've got a bloody cheek, having a telephone installed. Who pays for that, eh?" Michael held Gladys up off the floor by her clothes. Then he threw her down on the settee, stormed into the hallway, grabbed his coat, and left by the front door. Michael had gone to see his mother. Gladys was angry, walking around the house saying, "Bloody college indeed! What girls go to bloody college? What a waste that would be." Teresa went to her room thinking, "Well, not one of them asked me. Would I, or wouldn't I? Who knows? Wait and see. Neither of them would let me go to drama school years ago, which I would have loved. Is this another great opportunity missed? Why can't I progress and do things I love? I know I'm talented. Teachers have told them before, and after all, Terry has never had teachers tell them good things about him."

Meanwhile, Tabitha asked her, "What's going on? What are the arguments about?" Teresa replied, "They're over me, as usual," and she went to her room. Tabitha followed Teresa into her room and asked her, "Do you want to go to college?" Teresa replied, "I want to be an actress or a writer". She then went on to say, "I think I could do drama in college. I think I need to go if I want to be an actress." Tabitha gave Teresa a cuddle and said, "I feel so sorry for you." She then left and went downstairs to talk to her mother. Tabitha said, "Are you going to let Teresa go to college? She really wants to go. She wants to be an actress". "Gladys replied, "No, I can't afford for her to go. She's already interested in boys, and she's also been offered a full-time position in the supermarket when she leaves school." "Well," said Tabitha, "I think you're mean to Teresa". Gladys replied, "Mind your own business, Tabitha; it's nothing to do with you." Tabitha replied, "You're still mean," and she went to her room.

Later that evening, Michael returned home from his mother's. He approaches Gladys to say that his mother would help with any costs which may occur in college to support Teresa. Gladys was fuming! "Oh, here we go again, more interference from your mother." Michael replied, "You know how she feels about Teresa; she just wants the best for her". "The best?" replied Gladys. "Maybe she should go and live with her because she's just like her. You tell your mother to keep her nose out or I will break it for her." "That's right," replied Michael, "violence again with you, isn't it?" Gladys hit the roof. "Violence with me?" she replied. "You're the one who has beaten Teresa and me almost to death; trying to make amends, are you?" Michael held back his anger and went to the back room where he could get some peace. The following week whilst Teresa was in school, Mrs Bowden called her into her office and said, "Hello, Teresa. How are things at home? Have your parents decided on college?" Teresa said, "It has caused rows in the house, and Mother has said no, so I don't think I'm going to be allowed." "That's a shame, as this would be a marvellous opportunity for you. Have you got a telephone in your house?" Teresa replied. "Yes," and gave Mrs Bowden her telephone number. "That's all for now then, Teresa. I will give your parents a call." Later that day, Mrs Bowden telephoned. Michael answered the call and told Mrs Bowden, "If I had my way, Teresa would go, but her mother's totally against it." "So, your decision is final?" asked Mrs Bowden. Michael replied, "Sadly, yes. My life wouldn't be worth living if I went against Gladys's decision". "Okay," Mrs Bowden replied. "I think you are both making a big mistake," and she hung up the telephone. Unbeknown to Michael, Gladys had heard every word as she was on her way downstairs and she challenged Michael. "Your life wouldn't be worth living, would it? You're gutless not to say it was your decision also." "Well, it wasn't, was it?" replied Michael. Gladys flew into a rage and put her hands around Michael's throat saying, "I'm fed up with you! You're the reason she can't go because you never earn enough money!" Gladys continued slapping Michael until he could hold his temper no more and punched Gladys in the face, giving her a bleeding nose. Then, he said, "Now leave me alone. You only ever want the best for the golden child, Terry, don't you?" Michael went out into the garden slamming the back door behind him, and at that moment, Maisie was walking up the garden path and said hello to Michael. Michael turned and said, "She's in a bloody mood in there". "Why's that?" replied Maisie. "We had a row over Teresa going to college. Is Pamela going to college?" he asked. "No," Maisie said, "she hasn't had the chance; her exam results weren't as good as Teresa's, but if she did have the chance, both myself and Dan would support her, but you see, Michael, Pamela is an only child, isn't she?" Maisie walked into the house and saw Gladys holding her nose. Maisie comforted Gladys while she told her what happened. Maisie asked, "Has he been taking his tablets?" "I think so," replied Gladys. They both went into the front room with a cup of tea, just as Teresa walked in from school. Gladys attacked Teresa, accusing her of causing trouble regarding the school phoning, and Maisie took her side and said to Teresa, "You should be ashamed of yourself! If your mother says you can't go, you can't go and you should respect her decision." Michael came in from outside and heard Teresa upset and trying to defend herself. Both Gladys and Maisie were shouting at Teresa. Michael went into a rage, defended Teresa and ordered Maisie out of his house. Gladys said to Maisie, "Don't you go. It's my house and you're my friend; stay right where you are." Maisie said, "No, Gladys. I will call again when Michael is not here." Maisie left the house, giving Teresa a filthy look on her way out. Teresa, for the sake of a peaceful life, stayed out of her parents' way and went out as much as she could. Eventually, things calmed down over the next few weeks and the school term ended. College was never mentioned again by anyone. Teresa took a full-time position in the supermarket, but now and again, she wondered what might have been.

Tabitha loved having friends over; she was a right little teenager now, and growing in confidence still. Terry, still Mr Favourite, could do no wrong as always. Gladys made Teresa pay two pounds a week out of her six pounds ten shillings weekly wage, for her board and lodging, and told Teresa, "Terry is now paying too". Teresa never believed her, as Terry always had a smirk on his face. He used to spend and spend when he should have been saving for a car. Michael and Gladys promised they would help him, but he must put some money towards it himself. Deep down, Teresa always knew her dad was right - Terry was the favourite, and Gladys would do all in her power to defend and help him any way she could. Teresa thought to herself, "Never mind him. I'm strong and owe her nothing."

Chapter 3

Discrimination

Winter had arrived, and Teresa bought herself a coat and no longer relied on her parents for anything. She loved the independence working was giving her. She made a lot of friends at work and got to know a lot of the customers. This was a whole new world she had entered, and at only fifteen years old. She went into the house after finishing her work one day to see Tabitha very upset. Tabitha told her that her mother wouldn't buy her new clothes and shoes for her school Christmas party. Teresa replied, "She wouldn't buy mine either when I was in school. What was it you wanted exactly?" she asked Tabitha. Tabitha showed Teresa the outfit she liked in the catalogue, which a neighbour ran. Teresa went to the neighbour's house and ordered the outfit and new shoes for Tabitha. Tabitha was elated. Tabitha ran to her mother and said, "Teresa has bought my outfit. Not like you!" Gladys slapped Tabitha, and said, "When I say no, it's no." She then grabbed hold of Teresa and said, "How dare you go behind my back? If you can afford them then you can afford to pay more board and lodging." Teresa answered Gladys in a disrespectful way, saying, "If you didn't spend so much on nice clothes, high heels, and bags, we would have a better life." Of course, all this was true, as Gladys kept herself very smart, with loads of clothes, dresses, shoes and handbags. She always had a wardrobe full of clothes, as she and Maisie always went shopping together. Teresa then threw Terry up to Gladys saying, "His supposed board and lodging includes his clothes too, whereas mine is only board and food; I have to buy my own clothes. Why is that, Mother?" Gladys walked out of the heated discussion, glaring at Teresa; it was a look of hate.

In the following weeks, Gladys avoided any conversation with Teresa, but did say to Tabitha that she looked lovely in her party clothes and that she should thank her big sister. Teresa thought, "At least I had some recognition". Tabitha looked amazing in her new outfit, consisting of a black skirt and a white frilly blouse, then complemented with a black waistcoat to match. Her white shoes had a small heel and a black strap. Tabitha was searching her jewellery for something to match her clothes, but of course, it was Teresa's jewellery she needed once again.

Christmas came without arguments, which was nice, and all the family appeared to have a good time. After the holidays, Terry had his seventeenth birthday and asked Michael and Gladys for a car. Working in a garage, Terry would obviously want a car someday, but Michael hit the roof and told him, "I know you haven't saved anything towards it as you just spend your wages on rubbish. Also, there's plenty of time before buying a car." Teresa and Terry were in the kitchen when a massive row broke out; it was Gladys trying to persuade Michael to buy Terry a car. They heard Michael shout, "No way am I going to the bank for a loan for a car for Terry!" Then Gladys said, "You should do, as he is your only son and needs a car." "What about Teresa's college, and what about Tabitha's clothes? They are your daughters," replied Michael. Meanwhile, Terry said to Teresa, "I will get my car, you know. Mum will work on him because she knows I've noticed things." "What things?" Teresa asked, so Terry explained to Teresa that he thought Gladys was having an affair with Uncle Robert and told her to be more aware of their behaviour when Uncle Robert stayed. "Observe the little things, then tell me what you think," he told Teresa. The row in the room was escalating as the siblings listened in. The coffee table was turned over by Michael and his favourite ornament was thrown at him and smashed by his feet. Terry was laughing, but Teresa went upstairs to her room, but on her way, she spotted Tabitha on her way down. Teresa then told her, "Go back up, it's not safe. They're arguing again."

There was an atmosphere again in the house for weeks but things did seem to perk up when Uncle Robert arrived to stay, with both Gladys and Michael hiding the arguments well during his stay. Teresa did what Terry said to do; she watched and noticed. A day later, they were holding hands. "Oh, my God," she thought, "he must be right!" He had said this for years. Teresa reflected on years before, how they both stayed together all the time, when Robert would take Gladys shopping, the incident with the hot tea, the condom in the bedroom, how Gladys always looked her best when he arrived, and the secrets she was told by Gladys not to tell or share with anyone. "Are my thoughts running riot?" she asked herself. She really wasn't sure. One thing she was sure of was that she had seen them holding hands, so she was determined to stay vigilant while life trundled on.

Teresa continues to go to work and got a promotion to cashier. This meant more money as she had to be trained to cash up at night and handle the day's takings. She was great at this as her maths skills came in very useful for cashing up and giving the correct change. This promotion came with a pay rise of ten shillings a week. "How great is this?" she thought. "Now I can save more." Nevertheless, Gladys put her board and lodging up to two pounds and five shillings a week.

Whilst at work, she noticed that a boy came to her till with his father every Saturday. He always queued at her till. Teresa started to notice his winks, and the smile of his father. It now became obvious to Teresa that he liked her. He was quite short, not bad looking, and he had a lovely smile. One evening at home, the doorbell rang. Teresa answered the door as she was on her way downstairs. On the doorstep, standing there, was the same boy! Teresa could feel her colour going red and asked him what he wanted. "I've come to pick my sister up," he said. His sister was a friend of Tabitha's, so, Teresa went and fetched her, telling her that her brother had come to take her home. Every time Tabitha's friend Carol came to the house, her brother would always pick her up, and always made a point of seeing Teresa while hoping to talk to her. His name was James, and he drove a mini-Cooper, green with a white top, and with the loudest air horns you could imagine. They played a tune, which they always did when he left the house with his sister. On one trip, he asked Teresa if she would go out with him. Teresa accepted a date with James and soon began to see him most nights. However, Teresa still had to be in the house by eight-thirty pm. Teresa followed all the fashion; miniskirts, hot pants, midi skirts. maxi skirts, and flared trousers. She even had the footwear to go with them; knee-high boots, short boots, high heels. Teresa was turning into a very fashionable young lady, but at only sixteen, she was still much too young to settle down. She should be having fun with her friends, as they told her they were missing her. Teresa arranged to spend her next Saturday off with her friends, as James would only be doing the weekly shop with his father. James's mother had died when he was only a young boy, and he had four siblings, so a big family. Teresa got up out of bed on that Saturday morning, only to see Terry had a car and it wasn't a banger; this was a sporty newish car, a Ford Capri and not very old. Terry had got his way. "How did that happen?" she thought to herself. "He hasn't passed his test yet." But Michael put L-plates on the front and back of the car. Teresa rushed downstairs and asked Gladys, "How come he's got a car?" Gladys replied, "Because he needs one for his work." Teresa then retorted, "He hasn't even passed his test yet. How did he pay for that?" "None of your business," replied Gladys. Michael came in from the car and Teresa asked him the same question. Michael didn't know how to answer the question and looked at Gladys, saying, "I told you so," and walked off without giving an answer at all. Terry, smirking all over his face, was very pleased with himself. Teresa said to Terry, "Well, you got your own way, then, didn't you?" "Yes, of course," he replied. "Mum persuaded Dad to help me, didn't she? I told you this would happen, Teresa," he replied. Teresa went back upstairs to have a bath and passed Tabitha on the stairs. "How did he get that?" asked Tabitha. Teresa replied, "Golden child, isn't he?" Then she shut the door to the bathroom. Teresa, now ready to go out for the day with her friends, made her way downstairs, grabbed her coat and went out, slamming the door. Tabitha noticed Teresa wasn't happy about the car, so asked Michael and Gladys, "Are you going to buy Teresa a car next year and me one when I'm seventeen?" Gladys replied, "No, you're girls and mainly boys drive". Tabitha remembered the conversation between the siblings years ago when they met Uncle Robert and saw his car. "Terry said it would be like that, and he's right; wait until I tell Teresa," Tabitha thought to herself. Teresa was late coming home that night, and Gladys kept checking the front door, looking down the street for her. Michael said to Gladys, "She wasn't happy about the car". "She will get over it," replied Gladys with a 'couldn't care less' attitude. Tabitha butted in and said, "I'm going to tell her we aren't going to have a car, as it isn't fair." "Shut up," said Gladys. Life isn't fair; you sound like your sister." "Teresa has nothing, and neither do I," she replied. "It's always golden child Terry; he has everything he asks for." Michael stepped in and said to Tabitha, "Your mother and I made the decision, and you should not be questioning it. What we say is final." "We?" thought Tabitha. "They never join forces; what's going on here?"

One hour turned into two, then three… Gladys was fuming, as Teresa should have been in by eight-thirty. Michael went to bed as he knew there was going to be trouble, whilst Terry stayed up with Gladys. Tabitha was afraid for Teresa; therefore, she couldn't sleep, and was also looking out of the window with worry. Finally, a car came up the road and Teresa got out, with Elizabeth, still in the car, shouting "goodnight" to Teresa. Teresa had been to a barn dance and genuinely forgot the time, so she decided to stay till the end, as she would be in as much trouble for being an hour late as three hours late; "Late is late," she thought. Teresa was laughing as she got out of the car and walked towards her mother, Gladys, who was standing on the doorstep. Gladys took off her slipper and started hitting Teresa around her head and face saying, "Don't you do this to me again!" "Do what, you bitch?" said Teresa. "Having a life that's fun not violent isn't ok with you, is it, Mother?" she said. Teresa wasn't going to put up with this and pushed Gladys into the wall. Gladys was still lashing out at Teresa who was fighting back, which woke Michael. He rushed downstairs to stop the fighting. Terry was enjoying the fight between his mother and sister. Michael sent Teresa upstairs and then comforted Gladys. This was an action never seen by the siblings before; it was always them fighting.

Sunday morning arrived. Teresa phoned James to arrange to meet up earlier than before, as she never wanted to stay in the house, and she was adamant she wasn't going to do any chores either. "Gladys can do it herself for a change," were Teresa's thoughts. James beeped his car outside and Teresa was grabbing her bag and coat out of the hallway when her mother shouted, "Where do you think you're off to?" "None of your business," replied Teresa, and out she marched giving the door a jolly good slam on her way out. Teresa didn't go far, only to James's house, where she sat with his father and sister Carol. Teresa never spoke a lot about her family life, but James picked up on the pressure Teresa was under, therefore, he asked questions. A lot of questions. James's father Fred told James and Teresa that there was a room in the house that James could paint up and use as their room, especially when Teresa needed a place to go. "A sort of sanctuary," thought Teresa. She thought that would be good. James was very eager to start work on the room and was already asking Teresa about colours and wallpaper. Eight o'clock came and James drove Teresa home. He asked if he should go into the house with her. "No," replied Teresa as she never knew what kind of atmosphere she would be walking into. As she walked into the house, Michael and Gladys were both sitting on the settee very close together and totally ignored Teresa. Tabitha came out of the room to talk to Teresa and told her what their mum and dad had said about them having a car. "It's a definite no," she said. Teresa then told Tabitha about the room at James's house, a place where she could be away from them. Tabitha asked, "Can I come with you, Teresa?" Teresa replied, "If things get that bad for you, I will take you myself." "But you don't have a car," replied Tabitha, but Teresa knew she would one day, as she was practising driving James's mini around the field adjoining his house. "Don't worry about that, Tabitha. I will get you there somehow," replied Teresa.

Not liking the atmosphere, Teresa went to her room and sorted out clothes for work the following day. Gladys came upstairs and said to Teresa, "Seeing as you never did your chores today, your dirty clothes, and clothes that are needing ironing, are all waiting for you in the basket for you to do yourself." Teresa replied, "No problem. I will do my own," and with that, Gladys hit Teresa around the head, calling her a selfish, lazy bitch. Teresa couldn't help but react, saying, "What were you doing all day? Call me lazy, eh? What does golden child Terry do? I'll tell you what, Teresa. Continues to do bugger all, and by doing bugger all, he gets all he wants, doesn't he, Mother?" Teresa was very angry, and slammed her bedroom door in Gladys's face, keeping her out of her room. Tabitha's eyes and mouth were wide open; she couldn't believe what Teresa had said to her mother. Gladys marched back downstairs to tell Michael, but Michael had heard what Teresa said and, deep down, he knew it was the truth but very disrespectful. It was always Teresa, do this, Teresa, do that. Terry did nothing as he was a boy, and Tabitha, thirteen, was the baby of the family. Michael realised that Teresa had been doing the washing, ironing, and housework at a much younger age than Tabitha and wholeheartedly felt sorry for Teresa.

Weeks went by with Michael and Gladys still not fighting, even eating meals in the same room. Uncle Robert visited and started taking Terry out in his car, teaching him how to drive. It was months later when Terry passed his test. He was the big man now, even taking Gladys to do her shopping. He would always be polishing his car, and on numerous occasions, asked Teresa if she would hoover the inside and clean the windows. This Teresa always refused, then one day, he said, "You clean for Mum, etc, so why not clean my car? I'll pay you." But she still refused. The following day, as she was entering the house, there were raised voices coming from the kitchen. Uncle Robert, Gladys, and Michael were all in there. Teresa hung her coat up and listened outside the door; she soon noticed it was Michael who was raising his voice. He was saying to Gladys, "I'm better now. So, I'm going to try again". Gladys replied, "You will never be better, as you call it. You're still on medication." Teresa came to realise that Michael was on about buying a car for himself and driving again. Uncle Robert had taken Gladys's side, telling Michael there was no need for him to drive as he had his car and Terry had his. Michael never liked being told by his brother-in-law that he couldn't do something and felt Gladys wouldn't have argued with him if Uncle Robert hadn't been there. Michael said to them both, "Don't worry; I will do what I want, not what you say". He walked out of the kitchen and met Teresa in the hallway. Teresa said, "You okay, Dad?" Michael replied. "No, Teresa, I'm not. I'm bloody not." With that, he stormed back into his room. His peaceful room. Michael felt discriminated against, which he was, of course, and Teresa felt so sorry for Michael. He was being treated just like a child in his own home, being told what to do by his wife and brother-in-law. Teresa found these actions demoralising and hurtful. She wished she could do something or say something, but she couldn't find the right words or actions. Life could be cruel, this she was learning; sometimes it can't even be fixed, no matter how we try. Michael never mentioned the car again, just like he had given up on his dream of ever driving or becoming independent like Terry and Uncle Robert. Teresa just thought, "Maybe one day, we never know, things can change."

Chapter 4

The Accusation

It was a lovely spring morning and the sun was shining through the bedroom curtains, when Teresa's alarm went off, reminding her to get up and go to work. Life was back to normal regarding Michael and Gladys with the snide remarks back and forth between each other. Not a very nice atmosphere yet again. Terry went to work, as did Teresa, and Tabitha, with her school bag over her shoulder, went off to school. The postman delivered a letter addressed to Michael; he put it on the side while he made a cup of tea when Gladys entered the kitchen. She asked, "Why aren't you at work today?" "Holidays," replied Michael. He then took his cup of tea along with his letter into his room. The letter made Michael stand up and pace the room, reading it over and over; he was more than shocked. Gladys, meanwhile, was in the kitchen with her tea and biscuits, oblivious to all this. Michael walked out of his room and entered the sitting room. Gladys wasn't there, so he proceeded to the kitchen. He then waved the letter in front of Gladys's face. Michael said to Gladys, "Do you know who this is from?" Gladys replied, "What's the matter with you? How can I possibly know who it's from!" Michael went on to shout in Gladys's face, "It's from my sister Myfanwy, saying you and Robert are having an affair." Gladys turned white and denied everything that was in the letter. She said to Michael, "You should know me and Robert better than that. I am not having an affair." Michael didn't believe Gladys as Myfanwy had found red lipstick on his shirt, also a strong smell of perfume, both of which Gladys wore. In the letter, she stated that she would be confronting Robert that evening before they had time to talk, and to let Gladys know he wouldn't be staying at the house anymore during his visits with work.

The letter went on, telling Michael his wife was a slut, and that he should throw her out. Michael said to Gladys, "I've had my doubts all the time, and he definitely isn't staying in my house anymore." Gladys didn't like that and slapped Michael, who slapped her back, and the old words came out. "My mother was right about you; you are a moll!" Michael left the house, slamming the door behind him. Gladys, however, tried to telephone Robert, but couldn't get an answer. She only had one number, which was his main office. She couldn't track him down. Gladys sobbed and sobbed, not knowing what to do. Michael had gone to see his mother taking the letter with him. Uncle Ben told Michael, "Myfanwy does suffer with depression, so you must be sure before acting on this information". Michael told Uncle Ben, "I believe it to be true, and I have already confronted Gladys". Meanwhile, Nana Jane said, "Throw her out; she's never been good enough for you". Michael broke down crying, not knowing what to think. Uncle Ben gave Michael Myfanwy's telephone number and told him to go and phone Myfanwy from the telephone box at the end of the lane. Michael, checking his change, took the number and went down the lane to the telephone box. Michael was on the phone to Myfanwy for what seemed like an hour before he had to hang up as someone else wanted to use the telephone. Myfanwy told Michael that she had been watching Robert for a few years now, as she caught him on the telephone talking to someone but he wouldn't say who - "Just work, Myfanwy, just work," he'd reply. Michael was also surprised that Myfanwy didn't have his telephone number, so he gave it to her. Michael walked back to his mother's house, thinking out loud, saying, "No wonder he wanted the phone in my house, so they could talk together regularly. That's why Myfanwy wasn't told we had a phone put in". Michael was putting the pieces of the puzzle together. He truly believed it was the truth despite Gladys's denial. He walked back to his mother's house and told Uncle Ben and his mother about the conversation between Myfanwy and himself. Meanwhile, Gladys was still trying to get hold of Robert whilst Michael was out, but had no luck contacting him. Gladys made a cup of tea and smoked a cigarette to try and stop her hands from shaking, although she was still sobbing. Minutes later, the phone rang. She felt relieved and rushed into the hallway to answer it in the hope that it was Robert, but it was not. Gladys answered and was taken aback as she listened to a very angry Myfanwy saying, "How dare you go with my husband? You're no good. You are a nasty little slut.

He is a family man, or did you not know that? Are you really that stupid? You're a whore!" Still shaking, Gladys hung up and wondered how she had got her telephone number.

Time passed and Tabitha walked in from school and asked Gladys, "Why have you been crying? Had another row with Dad, have you?" Gladys replied, "No. Well, yes and no. I've been accused of doing something bad, which you must not ever believe if your father tells you about it, okay?" Tabitha said, "What must I not believe?" Gladys replied, "You're too young, Tabitha, you wouldn't understand". "Try me," said Tabitha. "Your auntie has accused me of having an affair with Uncle Robert," Gladys went on to say, "but it isn't true. You must believe that." Tabitha replied, "I know what an affair is, Mum, I'm not stupid". Gladys then told Tabitha, "Your father believes it and has stopped Uncle Robert from staying here". Tabitha wasn't at all interested, so went to her room completely unfazed. Later, Terry came home from work and Gladys told him the same. Terry prompted more information from Gladys and tried to comfort her. However, when Teresa came in, she saw Terry and Gladys talking, but went upstairs to change, only to be given the information by Tabitha. "Oh my god!" Teresa said. "Terry was right all the time. How unobservant and foolish are we, Tabitha?" Teresa felt sorry for Michael, as all the signs were there, and she had ignored them. "Should I have told all the secrets I was asked to keep as a child, and the sitting close and holding of hands? Am I a bad person?" All these questions went through Teresa's mind as she began to beat herself up. "Where is Dad now?" Teresa asked Tabitha. "I don't really know," she replied. "I bet he's gone to Nana Jane's," replied Teresa. "I'm not looking forward to tonight, Teresa. I'm more than a little afraid of what's going to happen. Will you please stay in with me?" Teresa had arranged to go out with James that night, but when she heard this, she said, "Of course. When James comes to pick me up, I will tell him it's best I stay in tonight." "Thank you," Tabitha replied.

Both girls went downstairs and put the television on, then Teresa went to the kitchen to make them both something to eat. Gladys was in the bathroom and Terry started telling all to Teresa, saying, "I told you so. I knew it, didn't I?" "Then why are you comforting Mother then if you're sure she's guilty?" asked Teresa. "Well," replied Terry, "I've got to protect her from

Dad when he gets in, haven't I?" "No," said Teresa. "He's done no wrong, has he? Do you know where he is?" "No," replied Terry, "but he better not start on her when he does get here." Teresa thought to herself, "Billy Big Head is on guard. Happy days." Teresa went back into the room, meeting her mother in the hallway. Gladys warned her, "Your father won't be himself when he gets in. Take no notice of what he says because it's all lies". Teresa replied, "Is it now? You're telling me what to think now, are you?" Gladys replied, "Trust you to be awkward". Teresa then replied, "No, Mother, I'm just honest". Gladys shrugged her shoulders and returned to the kitchen, where she had support from Terry; total support from Terry.

Hours passed by and there was no sign of Michael. All the family went to bed, but during the early hours, Terry, Teresa, and Tabitha were woken up by a fight in their mother's bedroom. It wasn't just a fight, it was very violent, just like when they were children. Terry went into the bedroom and punched Michael. Michael was in such a rage he had the strength to hold Terry back, pushing and punching him out of the room. Terry was on the landing floor bleeding; Tabitha, although a teenager, hid behind Teresa who was behind the bedroom door, and, just like years ago, she wet herself and started shaking. Teresa stayed put with Tabitha behind her crying and screaming. Gladys comes out and she was also bleeding. Michael made his way downstairs, looked to Teresa and said, "You and Tabitha are the only good ones in this family, Teresa; I do love you."

Teresa was tending to her mother when there was a knock on the door; Terry had called the police. Michael was shaking at the bottom of the stairs when Terry opened the door and let them in. The police came upstairs and called an ambulance for Gladys. Her injuries were bad; she could hardly walk and was covered in blood. All her hair was also matted with blood. Michael started crying and told the doctor and the police that he had a cheating wife - "She's no good," he kept saying, "she's no good." A police-woman started to question all three siblings and called Maisie, the family friend, to stay with them. Terry and Gladys were both taken to hospital. Gladys had stitches in her head. Michael was taken to the same hospital where he went before when they were younger. Terry had a bleeding nose and two black eyes. He was shaken up, as was Gladys. Both returned home early in the morning, but no thought was given to Tabitha, who couldn't stop shaking. She hadn't grown in confidence as we previously thought, and Teresa was still her protector. Over the coming weeks, Tabitha was taken to the doctors, and they told Gladys she was suffering with her nerves. From that day, she very rarely went to school. There was always a genuine reason why - bad stomach, afraid to go out - just anything not to attend school. And thinking back, Teresa thought she had suffered most when there were fights, but had always had Teresa to hold her hand when going to school. That was when Tabitha was most confident, when she had Teresa in school, as she was never alone.

Gladys attended the hospital to see Michael and have discussions about his treatment. Once again, Michael needed to have ECT treatment for his nerves, as once again, he'd had a nervous breakdown. Terry was her taxi back and forth, and Robert was nowhere to be seen. Teresa partly blamed him and Gladys for Michael's breakdown. One day, after the hospital visit, the phone rang and Teresa answered it. It was Nana Jane wanting to know how her son was, as Gladys had told the hospital it was because of her that he'd had his breakdown. Doctors called it a mother complex. Teresa called to her mother, saying, "It's Nana Jane. Do you want to talk to her?" "No," said Gladys, but then said, "Yes, I do". Gladys went to the phone, then Teresa heard her say to Nana Jane, "You caused this, filling his head with all sorts. Do you realise what happened when he came home that night? Do you? Don't inquire again and just so that you know, you are not allowed to see him in the hospital. Goodbye!" Gladys then hung up the phone. No visitors came to the house this time, only Maisie, Gladys's friend. Unbeknown to the children, however, Gladys was in regular contact with Robert. Was there truth in the accusation Teresa wondered? She then thought "Yes, it was the truth, but it has all been twisted back to Nana Jane and Auntie Myfanwy's depression, according to Gladys and Robert."

Weeks went by, with Gladys at the hospital every day and Uncle Robert denying everything to Myfanwy and telling her she had caused her brother's breakdown. Myfanwy knew she saw what she saw, and smelt what she smelt, and Robert had no explanation as to why the perfume and lipstick marks were on his clothes. He accused Myfanwy of being untrusting, and not liking Gladys, as she just jumped to the wrong conclusion, but Myfanwy defended herself by saying to Robert, "What other conclusion is there, Robert?" Later that week, Myfanwy answered her telephone and it was a lady from Robert's work. Robert wasn't in so she asked to take a message. "It's just a massive thank you to him for arranging my leaving party at the office a couple of weeks ago." She then went on to say, "Could you ask him to ring me on this telephone number, please? I would like to thank him personally and he would want to know how I'm getting on." Myfanwy took her telephone number and assured the lady she would pass on the message.

Myfanwy did pass on the message to Robert and started to doubt her actions. The party was weeks ago. Robert always worked away, and she couldn't possibly know which shirt Robert had worn on which day. Myfanwy asked Robert "Did you attend the office party? The one you arranged for that lady?" Robert replied, "Yes, I did; it was a surprise party for her. Just cake, wine, and all office colleagues. It was held after working hours, but in the office, because such a special lady deserved an after-work leaving party. I will ring her now before I forget," he replied. Myfanwy listened in and realised it was all professional. She began to doubt herself - "Was I wrong? How could I be? I've suspected this for years. I wouldn't make my brother have a nervous breakdown on a whim." Myfanwy couldn't remove the doubt she had. So, she carried on convincing herself she was right with her actions. Robert continued to book bed and breakfast accommodation whenever he worked away, and never once stayed at Michael and Gladys's house.

The day came when Michael was discharged from hospital. None of the children had visited him during his stay; the doctors had advised against it as they wanted Michael to reflect without distraction. A different Michael returned home. He was calm and smiling. "I'm glad to be home," he said to all who asked. He asked Gladys to bring all the three siblings to him as he wanted to talk to them. Terry, Teresa, and Tabitha went into the lounge to see what their father had to say. "Firstly, I want to apologise to you, Terry, as I know you were only defending your mother. I'm very, very sorry, but you all know why I went a bit crazy." Terry said nothing. Michael then turned to Teresa and apologised once again. He pleaded with Tabitha, "Please, don't be afraid of me, I would never hurt you". Tabitha also said nothing. Knowing Tabitha was also now on nerve medication, he went on to say, "We are both on tablets but mine are much stronger now, Tabitha, so you have nothing to fear, and you will also get better". Teresa doubted that Tabitha would get better as she was just so nervous. She still wouldn't go to school, or out anywhere, come to that. Life went on with the family tiptoeing around Michael, trying not to say the wrong thing, or to trigger another breakdown. It was like walking on glass or eggshells, as the saying goes.

Chapter 5

Moral Expectations

Just like the rest of the family, Teresa carried on with life as best she could. Michael went back to work once again, and Terry was more than halfway through his apprenticeship. Teresa worked during the day and went out with James in the evening, but Tabitha was still not attending school. Gladys was not bothered about it, as it was company for her when the rest of the family was at work. One Friday evening, Gladys asked Terry and Teresa if they would stay at home on Saturday as she wanted their support. Gladys wanted them to understand that their father had been speaking to Uncle Robert and Auntie Myfanwy, and they had concluded it was all a misunderstanding. They had put the past behind them and decided it was the best way forward. Therefore, they were coming to visit. Gladys looked at all the siblings and said to Terry in particular, "You must not ask questions about the past couple of months. You must all be polite and make them welcome." "But look at the trouble Myfanwy caused," said Terry. Then Teresa said, "Bet Uncle Robert is happy!" and surprisingly, Tabitha said, "Oh, here we go again, then". "That's enough," replied Gladys. "I know you have all got your own opinions on them, but it's your father's decision." None of the siblings were happy about the situation, especially Terry and Teresa. Could they just put their feelings aside? They were both dreading the day. In the meantime, Gladys instructed Teresa to help with cleaning the house, and asked Terry to take her shopping. Saturday morning came and the visitors were due at about two pm. Gladys and Tabitha were preparing food in the kitchen, whilst Terry and Teresa were upstairs staying out of the way. After a while, Teresa ventured downstairs for a drink, only to find Gladys dolled up like a dog's dinner, including having her heels on, dancing to music in the dining room with Tabitha. Teresa thought, "Who's she trying to impress? Does she think she's a teenager now?" A not-so-happy and confused Teresa went back upstairs and said to Terry, "Seen what's going on down there?" "No," said Terry. "Only music on; wake up," said Teresa. "When is there ever music on downstairs? Never," she said, "only upstairs with us."

Teresa, not in a very good mood, didn't come downstairs to welcome the visitors until she was called. Terry just said "hello" in a frosty manner. Teresa, though, just nodded and went to make a cup of tea for all as instructed. Robert and Myfanwy brought with them a massive hamper and alcohol. They cried and hugged each other, very tightly, then they talked for hours. Then, after the food had been served, Teresa said to Gladys, "I'm going out with James". When Myfanwy asked, "Who's James?" Gladys replied, "Oh, it's a boy Teresa has been going out with for a year now. It is about that, isn't it, Teresa?" Teresa replied, "Yes, that's right." Not long after Teresa left, Terry made his excuses and did the same. On her return at nine o'clock, half an hour late for the eight-thirty rule, the visitors were still there, and Myfanwy said to Teresa, "You are a decent girl, keeping decent hours, and your mother says you never go to pubs. I'm glad of that, as no decent girls will ever be found in a pub." Teresa just smiled and went to watch TV.

For the next couple of months, they were all new best friends, and it was decided that Robert could stay again whilst working in the area. Michael was elated as everything was back to normal and he had missed the help Robert gave him about the house, and the money he gave them for lodging there. All was calm; Michael was taking his medication, as was Tabitha. One evening, Teresa was getting ready to go out with James, and as she came down the stairs, Michael commented on how beautiful she looked, and how proud of her he was. She entered the kitchen where James was talking to Gladys, and all went quiet, so she asked, "What are you talking about?" "Nothing," replied Gladys. James, however, had the biggest smile on his face and led Teresa out of the house. "There's something going on, James; what is it?" "It's a big surprise, Teresa. I can't say." All kinds of thoughts went around in her head; it was obviously something to do with her parents. It wasn't her birthday; Teresa didn't have a clue.

Approximately two weeks went by, then James came to pick her up as usual, and everyone was in the living room talking. Teresa came downstairs only to see James get down on one knee and propose to her. A very shocked Teresa said nothing. James then put the ring on her finger. Everyone was clapping and Gladys brought out the alcohol to raise a glass to the newly engaged couple. "Newly engaged?" thought Teresa. "I haven't even said yes to him." Gladys then went on to say, "We will have a party on Saturday. James, invite all your friends and family; you too, Teresa, invite your friends and workmates." The party was to be held in the house the following Saturday. Teresa thought, "I'm only seventeen; do I love him? What is love anyway? Maybe I do. I really don't know. And I never said yes. He never gave me a chance to answer him before he put the ring on my finger." Teresa got in the car, hardly speaking to James, but she couldn't help but hear him planning their future, this, that, and the rest of it. James took Teresa to his house, where he told his father Fred and his sister Carol. Fred hugged them, as did Carol, then Fred said to them both, "If you're stuck for somewhere to live, you can live here with us as you've already got your own room". James took Teresa by the hand and went into their room. He was planning a big redecoration to make it more homely. Teresa had a massive feeling of doubt and insecurity. "What's happening to me?" she asked herself. "He's the only boy I've ever known; more a friend, maybe?" She was very confused. The next day, Teresa went to work and told two of her best friends there. They looked at her engagement ring and congratulated her. Jean and Molly accepted the engagement party invitation. Jean said to Teresa, "You're only seventeen; hope this is a long engagement? I'm twenty-one and I don't want to settle down or have kids till at least twenty-five". Molly agreed with Jean saying to Teresa, "You're far too young for marriage, Teresa, please think on, and drag out this engagement; even have some fun and have a life first." Teresa knew they were right in what they said, and, feeling much better after talking to her friends, Teresa decided that it was not worth getting upset over, but to enjoy it and drag it out, and there was always the option to call it off as she hadn't said yes anyway.

Michael and Gladys were planning the party and Tabitha was excited. Terry was planning on having her room but with no success as Tabitha was still there. "Oh, my God," thought Teresa, "they think I'm going to have a short engagement and leave home very soon." Teresa told Terry that she was planning on a very long engagement, and he would be leaving before her.

Terry replied, "That's not Mum's intentions". Teresa replied, "Well, these are my intentions, so get used to it, and keep your beak out." Tabitha followed Teresa into the kitchen and said, "I want you to leave, because you'll have your own house and I can come to stay, then I won't have to stay here either then." Teresa, fully understanding of Tabitha's situation, knew that James wouldn't approve of that, as she didn't bother with his sister Carol anymore. Tabitha was afraid to go out on her own at all now, so she was not going to be making friends any time soon. Time went fast and Saturday soon came, and the so-called party began. There was no music, no dancing, just general chit-chat, cards, and gifts. Altogether, there was Gladys, Michael, Uncle Robert, Fred, Carol, Jean, Molly, Elizabeth, Terry, Tabitha and of course James and Teresa. Everyone sat down to sandwiches and cake. "This was no party," Teresa thought. "The only really happy people were all the parents." Fred was discussing living arrangements, and Gladys the wedding. Teresa felt overcome and quite frightened as her life was being planned. She left the room and joined her friends in the kitchen, having a cigarette by the back door. Teresa smoked more than usual and felt she was trapped. "What should I do?" she asked Molly. Molly replied, "It is worse than I thought, Teresa; you mustn't let this happen". Hugging her to console her, Jean said, "Please, Teresa, speak to James and see how he feels. Maybe he wants to wait longer and get his own place; you shouldn't live with in-laws anyway, so you must put a stop to all this." "Yes, but how do I do that? I feel it's what James wants anyway." "Look at yourself, Teresa," Molly said. "Your beautiful long hair, your slim figure, your lovely caring soul - I bet James wants this in case he loses you to someone else." Teresa knew they were right about anyone else stealing her as she has loads of wolf whistles from boys, and had been asked out on numerous occasions, but how could she plan her own life in a different direction?

Although engaged, she still had to be in the house at eight-thirty pm. James picked her up every night, so she couldn't make plans to go out with friends. Elizabeth, however, was in a serious relationship, and she also hadn't heard of the others in such a long time. Most probably, they were enjoying themselves at the barn dances, and the Saturday dances at the Town Hall. "I have been missing all this, but I wouldn't have been able to stay out with them anyway," she thought. With the party coming to an end, Teresa and

James thanked the guests for their cards and presents, then later, Teresa tried to talk to James in the hallway, when she was interrupted by her mother telling her, "Time for James to go now, Teresa. Kiss him goodnight, please." James laughed and said to Teresa, "Your life and mine will be better when you're out of here. Think about it, Teresa, no eight-thirty curfew." James then left taking Fred and Carol with him. Teresa went into the sitting room and her mother said, "Teresa, you have nice gifts here for your bottom drawer. We must think where to put them as you may be adding to them weekly if you're sensible." Teresa said nothing and made her way into the kitchen.

In the kitchen, Tabitha had started the washing up, so Teresa grabbed a tea towel to dry the dishes. Tabitha said to her, "Me and Carol have made up now, and she's coming here with James every evening to see me, and we're going out." "Where are you going?" asked Teresa. "We are just going out, down the shops and maybe town as well," said Tabitha. Teresa was pleased as she thought Tabitha had got some of her confidence back, and she knew Carol would like it because living out in the country, there was nothing to do and no one around; it could be a very lonely place. Gladys walked into the kitchen and Tabitha told her she was going out every night with Carol. Gladys replied, "Oh no, you're not going anywhere, my girl". Tabitha replied, "Yes, I am, and you can't stop me," and with that, she stormed upstairs. Gladys shouted, "We will see. We will see." Teresa was shocked at her little sister's confidence and cheek, chuckling to herself as she put the dishes away. The following day being a Sunday, James always picked Teresa up around three o'clock in the afternoon, and sure enough, there was Carol with him. Tabitha was dressed up, makeup also put on, looking quite grown up as she grabbed her coat. Gladys shouted to Tabitha, "Where do you think you're going?" Tabitha replied, "Out!" and shut the door. James then shouted from his car, "It's alright, she's only out with my sister; she'll be fine." Gladys just nodded and shut the front door. What Gladys didn't see was the way they were dressed and had makeup on, which made them look a lot older than they were. Teresa smiled to herself and thought, "Go, sis, go, but next time, don't steal my clothes and makeup!" Teresa and James dropped Tabitha and Carol off at the shops, and Teresa went with James to his house. They returned to her house at eight-thirty, and whilst talking to each other in the car, they noticed a group of boys and girls in the bus shelter down the road. It was then James realised it was Carol kissing a boy and Tabitha was there too. He started the car and drove to the bus stop, then told the girls to get home as he was leaving in half an hour. This they did, waiting for James and Teresa as they sat on the wall outside the house laughing. They were very happy. Teresa got out of the car and called to Carol to get in, then James and Carol drove off. Tabitha said, "I'm not going in without you. What did Mum say when I left?" "Nothing," replied Teresa, then she and Tabitha went into the house and hung their coats up in the hall. Teresa made her way to her room with Tabitha in tow, heading for the bathroom. "I'm not going in there," Tabitha said, pointing to the living room. Gladys heard them and came upstairs after them, calling to Tabitha, "Did you enjoy yourself tonight, Tabitha?" She replied, "Yes, thanks, Mum," as she was quickly trying to wash her makeup off. Gladys waited outside the bathroom door for her. When Tabitha came out, Gladys said, "Look on your bed, Tabitha, and you will see your school uniform. You're back to school tomorrow. If you can go out, you can go to school." "No, I'm not," replied Tabitha." Yes, you are, my girl; you will be going," said Gladys. Teresa looked at Tabitha and said, "Why don't you want to go now that you're friends again with Carol? Surely, it's better than being home with Mother?" Teresa went on to explain, "It's not that bad, Tabitha. You have more friends in school, and you appeared to be having fun tonight with the others". Tabitha was left thinking about what to do, as her mother wouldn't let her out tomorrow if she didn't go to school. Teresa wondered, was this the push Tabitha needed? She truly hoped so.

The following morning, Teresa got up, only to find Tabitha was in her uniform, and Gladys was ready to accompany her and talk to the teachers. Tabitha fitted right back in with her friends and appeared to enjoy her school days, and more so, the evenings out with Carol and other friends. Teresa was very happy that her sister had come out of her shell and realised that the engagement party had really helped Tabitha, as she was no longer at home every day. Gladys decided to go out to work and got herself a job cleaning in a large store part-time during the day. Also, Terry finished his apprenticeship and was working as a trained mechanic in the local garage. Anyone would think all should be happy in the house, but everything was set to get argumentative once again. Gladys kept on at Teresa to set a date for the wedding. She told her she should get her morals right, as it was the decent thing to do. Teresa never liked the discussion; she was following her friend's advice and avoided the subject as much as she could. Tabitha, however, was quite the little Madam, demanding new clothes, and stealing Teresa's without asking. Teresa gave her lots of clothes and makeup all the time. Michael could do nothing right according to Gladys and preferred his own company in his room as usual. However, he did continue taking his medication, whereas Tabitha had stopped completely! The new life Tabitha was leading was doing her good, especially getting her out of the house.

Teresa, still working in the supermarket as a cashier, had to go away for three days with work. She had to learn all about the new money which was coming in. Decimalisation was due to come in on the 15th of February, 1971. Funny money, people called it, but everyone in Britain had to learn it as this was the new legal currency. "Yes," thought Teresa. All her friends from work attended the training and stayed in a bed and breakfast paid for by the supermarket. They looked on this as a paid holiday, as being away from home was fantastic. They were in a city with lots of pubs, cafés, dance halls and cinemas, and there were parties happening most nights on the very long beach, and anybody could join in. Teresa, Jean and Molly would quickly return to the bed and breakfast after training to get changed. They would then join other girls whom they met on the training course and have a ball in the evenings. They would join hands, making a line, blocking the promenade, singing songs, going to bars, and dancing until the early hours of the morning. They were just having so much fun and Molly shouted to Teresa, "Teresa, this is what I meant by get a life first and have fun." Teresa's generation were classed as the defiant ones, with protests everywhere, disagreeing with laws and boundaries. These women were the trouble-seekers fighting for their rights. "If my mother could see me now," thought Teresa, "she would disown me, but she never saw so that's okay." The following morning, everybody had a test and had to prove they had learnt everything they were taught. The test was difficult, but all Teresa's colleagues scored top marks. They then spent the rest of their last day sightseeing and feeling quite sad as they had to leave. The journey home took a few hours, but all the girls were still laughing and promising that they must meet up and do it again sooner rather than later. "Oh, I do so wish," thought Teresa, "but all good things must come to an end".

PART III

Chapter 1

The Explosion

Everything was changing, just as Teresa had said, as this is the decade of The Beatles, Tom Jones, Cliff Richards, Flower power, Hippies, drugs, and freedom. But Teresa wasn't free; she was returning home from her training course. And she was completely oblivious, to what was going on at home. Nana Jane rang the house telling Michael, "Uncle Ben is very ill, and I need you here with me when the doctor arrives." On arrival at the house, Michael was led by his mother to the back room where a very ill Uncle Ben was lying on the sofa with a blanket over him. The doctor arrived and examined Ben then called for an ambulance. He told Jane, "Ben has an advanced case of pneumonia and needs to go to hospital immediately." Jane rushed to pack a bag for Ben, with his pyjamas, toiletries and his medication. Michael was holding Ben's hand but not making sense of anything he was trying to say, as he was just making a faint slurring noise. The ambulance arrived and they put Ben on the stretcher and gave him oxygen for the trip to hospital. Jane and Michael accompanied Ben, holding his hands and comforting him as he was confused and frightfully ill. They arrive at the hospital only to be told by the doctor that Ben wouldn't make it; he was dying. Michael phoned Gladys and was crying so hard he could hardly tell her the bad news. "This is the man I have known all my life; I love him like the father I never had," he explained to Gladys. Michael stayed with his mother next to Ben's bedside for two days and nights until Ben passed away. An inconsolable Michael left the hospital and accompanied his mother home. When they arrived back at the house, they made a cup of tea and sat talking about Ben. Michael was distraught, as was Jane. Michael said to Jane, "I wish I had understood what he was trying to say to me before the ambulance arrived. It was so faint, but I'm sure he was trying hard to talk to me". Jane said, "I know what he was trying to say to you, Michael." "What?" he asked. "He was trying to tell you he was your father, something he had wanted to tell you for years," she said. "What?!!" said Michael in shock. "You are telling me this now, when I always thought my father was the man who was bringing up my siblings miles away! So, my sisters aren't my sisters, are they?" Jane replied, "They are your half-sisters. I had to tell you. I was a housekeeper for Ben, and your sisters and father visited in order to avoid a scandal. I was having an affair with Ben when I fell pregnant with you. It wasn't accepted in those days and abortion was illegal then; it was a criminal offence. The girls' father, Norman, threw me out, so I came to live with Ben".

At that moment, Michael hated Jane and thought, "Why would she not let Ben tell me he was my father?" A very confused and upset Michael couldn't look at his mother. "You disgust me!" he said and walked out of the house. Michael then walked down the hill and into the pub at the bottom where he ordered a pint of Guinness, sat down and started thinking. Did the others know? If only he knew, he would have been different to Ben maybe, but he loved him as a father anyway. Also, their conversations would have been more like father and son instead of uncle and nephew. Michael didn't know what to think, but he was hurting, knowing Ben would never hear him call him Daddy or Dad as he got older. When he got home, he told Gladys, but she could not console him. His mind was spinning so he phoned Myfanwy and asked her if she knew. "Yes, I knew", she replied. "Listen to me, Michael, you were born when mother was in her forties and on the change of life; I am over twenty years older than you. We were all told by my father to call you our little brother, and pretend my father, Norman, was yours; this was to protect Jane's reputation. Ben was courting a nurse and about to settle down when Jane told him she was pregnant. Father took us to visit you and Jane to make people believe she was a live-in housekeeper. But no matter what, you are our little brother." Michael was processing all this new information and tried to explain it to Gladys. Gladys went mad, saying, "She calls me horrible names, knowing what she did was unforgivable and the lowest any woman can stoop. Adultery was never accepted in those days, and to walk out on all her other children, and her poor husband. Pretending you were his son to people, how cruel, oh my God, Michael, who is she? If this was to have got out then, she would have been socially outcast by all decent people.

You haven't even taken his surname." Michael was thinking if only he could turn back time, but he couldn't; he wanted to tell him how he felt. He had such a feeling of pride, as Ben was such a lovely gentleman to all who knew him. He always dressed smartly with his checked shirts, and was never seen without his waistcoat, which used to house his pocket watch. Now, it was too late for that; too late for everything. Gladys wanted to give her a piece of her mind, but she thought now was not the time. "But as they say, every dog has his day." Meanwhile, Michael said to Gladys, "By rights, I am a bastard, and Mother was a loose married woman. Obviously, she couldn't handle married life with Norman, who was a coal miner, and who lived in a small mining village. How lucky was she? He helped save her reputation. Also lucky, as Ben was a bachelor who owned his own house."

Teresa had now returned home from training for the decimalisation day. Gladys sat the siblings down and explained what had gone on regarding Uncle Ben dying, and Nana Jane's frivolous past. All three siblings felt sorry for Michael as he was in shock over his mother's behaviour. Teresa added, "Who the hell was she to tell me about morals and how a lady should behave? Honestly, who in their right minds would walk out on their children?" Teresa could never condone her nana's actions. She then went on to say, "And to withhold information as important as that from Dad. I hate the deceitful lying cow." Terry just sat back and said, "Well, she wasn't the lady we thought she was, and look how she used to call Mum a trollop, a whore and lots of other offensive names." Tabitha then asked, "Well, they weren't married, her and Uncle Ben then?" "No," replied Gladys, "but just support your dad through this traumatic time. Please, all of you?" Meanwhile, Michael was sitting in the armchair in the lounge, sobbing. Everyone left him alone to enable him to think and let everything sink in. The telephone rang and it was Minnie, saying that she and Myfanwy were coming down, and they would be at Nana Jane's house if Michael needed them. The message was passed on to Michael by Gladys, but he just ignored it. "Well, for now, maybe," she thought. Now, Michael had to decide if he could forgive his mother after she dropped that bombshell on him. Would it have been better if she had said nothing? After all, over forty years had passed. Or should she have done the right thing and told him earlier? Especially as Ben wanted him to know. But did Jane give Ben his last wish? No matter the consequences, Michael was sure that his father, Ben, was trying to tell him himself.

Later, the doorbell rang. Terry answered it. There stood Myfanwy, Minnie, and Nana Jane. Michael heard them and invited them into the sitting room. Gladys came in from the back garden and was more than surprised that Michael had invited them in. Gladys was in uproar as she had her reasons to confront Jane, personal ones, and she never wanted her in her house at all. But Teresa had taken them in tea and biscuits and made them feel welcome as she thought it was just what her father would have wanted. They all hugged and cried. Later, Myfanwy came out of the room to speak to Gladys, saying, "We need to talk, Gladys". Myfanwy then went on to say, "Michael had the better life out of all of us siblings. We were made to look after our father and our younger sisters without a mother, and it was hard, Gladys." She then went on to say, "He was only a coal miner who earned very little money to support all us girls, and sadly, our younger sister died, so please, Gladys, try to understand our circumstances growing up." Myfanwy then said, "You see, Gladys, I became the mother of our family at the very young age of twenty-three. I was courting Robert at the time Mother left us, and my father refused to bring up another man's child. He couldn't even afford it anyway." Gladys then had a light-bulb moment and shouted out loud, "You mean, Robert knew as well?" "Yes, he did, Gladys. He helped me pick up the pieces for my father after she had left." Myfanwy then continued saying, "She had to leave, Gladys; she had brought shame on our family. We couldn't risk that. So, we had to do as we were told and visit regularly. Sometimes we hated her and Michael, as they weren't in poverty like we were, but she was the only mother we had, and that, we must respect, no matter what. Besides, it was what Norman wanted. Norman never wanted us to be without our mother. So, when people asked, we told them she was working away to earn extra money, and she had taken our baby brother with her. And every now and again, she would come back to visit us, just for the neighbour's sake of course. Ben wanted Michael to know from the beginning as he was his only child and knew that Jane was too old to have any more children. Plus, he wanted the grandchildren to know him as Grampa, not Uncle Ben." Gladys then said, "Well, what about all the name-calling? Honestly, Myfanwy, you would never believe the things she's called me over the years and to find this out now - how hypocritical is that, eh?" "Yes, I agree," said Myfanwy, "but the past is the past, and this is the future. Let's all try and go forward from here if we can, please?" Winnie then entered the conversation saying, "I came out of the sitting room as I felt they needed to talk alone. I am welcome here, Gladys, aren't I?" Gladys assured Minnie that she was more than welcome and put the kettle on. Michael was in the sitting room for hours, talking and crying with his mother. The children went about their own business quietly whilst the visitors were there. It was late in the evening before the visitors left, then Gladys, like the children, went upstairs to bed. Gladys couldn't talk at all to Jane; therefore, Michael showed them out of the house. Jane did notice this but said nothing.

The funeral was planned to take place in four days' time. Ben worked in a beer factory just down the hill from where he lived. He was a very popular gentleman who was very well-liked by all his colleagues, so there was going to be a massive turnout. Michael and Gladys decided only they were going to attend, as they thought the children didn't need the experience of a funeral at such a young and vulnerable age. Meanwhile, Michael was back and forth to his mother's house, finishing off the arrangements. He seemed a lot calmer on the outside, but troubled on the inside. He wasn't sleeping, and he paced the house, mumbling to himself, which nobody really understood. Teresa asked, "Is Dad okay?" Gladys replied, "I'm not sure. I'm not even sure if he has taken any medication since he escorted Uncle Ben to hospital. Quite honestly, Teresa, I'm worried about him. Only he knows what's going on in his head, but I will be glad when the funeral is over, for his sake and ours."

On the day of the funeral, Terry and Teresa went off to work and Tabitha went to school just like any other day. Teresa wondered if anyone would be home when they got home, as the funeral wasn't until two pm, then the guests were all going back to Nana Jane's house for refreshments. She felt a little worried and sick inside as she knew Tabitha would be first home, but didn't know why she felt like this. "Oh, my God, I hope it's not a premonition," she thought. Was she overthinking things? Teresa had overheard her father say to her mother to be careful what she said at the funeral. Michael wanted his father to have a good trouble-free day for his send-off to heaven. Teresa knew he had pulled out all the stops for his father, even insisting he had the words 'good father to Michael' put on his headstone, which obviously couldn't be fitted until weeks later. Michael felt deeply that Ben would be looking down on him and enjoying the recognition he so desperately wanted from his son.

It was four pm, and Teresa was thinking about Tabitha, whilst wishing the next hour away so she could leave work and go home. The last hour dragged and dragged for her until finally, five o'clock arrived. Teresa grabbed her coat and caught the bus home that day as she was more than in a hurry. As she walked up the road to the house, all seemed quiet and when she reached the house, Tabitha opened the door to her. "You're early," said Tabitha. "Yes, I caught the bus up," she said. Terry wasn't home, but he didn't usually finish until six on a weekday. However, the relief Teresa felt was amazing, and the butterflies in her stomach had finally disappeared. "What on Earth was I worrying about?" she thought. Time dragged on and there was no sign of the parents, so they decided to go ahead and make themselves some food. James came later to call for Teresa, but she had a sinking feeling when he wanted her to go out. "Can we stay in this evening?" Teresa asked James. "Why is that?" he replied. "I've just got a feeling about going out tonight," she replied. "I don't want to leave Tabitha tonight, as she's not going out either, and it is the day of the funeral." Why don't we put the television on and let's see what's on tonight?" she asked James. This he did, and all three watched television. Terry came in and went to the pantry then took his food upstairs to his room. Hours passed, then Gladys came home; she was alone. Robert had given her a lift as Myfanwy, Minnie, and himself were leaving for home. Terry came downstairs and asked Gladys, "Where's Dad?" "He decided to stay behind longer with his mother," she replied. Teresa then asked, "Is everything okay with him?" "I don't bloody know, Teresa; how the hell would I? He's already offended a lot of people, including his sisters, so I got out of there." Teresa then thought to herself, "I knew something wasn't right – I've felt it all day long". "How long do you think he'll be then?" asked Teresa. "Stop asking questions. He's been drinking, drinking, and drinking a lot so I really don't know. Hopefully, he will stay out all night." Gladys, looking very smart in her black clothes, made herself a cup of tea, and sat at the kitchen table looking troubled and angry. James told Teresa that he was leaving for home, said goodnight to the rest of the family, and, as he got into his car, he shouted to Teresa, "You know where I am if you need me." She wondered why he would say that, but then he had obviously picked up on the atmosphere in the house and Teresa's butterflies had returned. Teresa went back into the kitchen to speak to Gladys, making small talk; "Were there lots of people at the church?" she asked. "The church was full, and there were still lots of people outside," she told Teresa. Gladys was quite calm but reserved, obviously worried and concerned about Michael. So, Teresa went to bed and joined Tabitha. Terry was in his room. Gladys locked the doors and went to bed, as she never knew when or even if, Michael would be home that night. In the early hours of the morning, Gladys was awakened by a commotion outside. It was Michael and a strange man. Michael was shouting at the top of his voice. "I am not Mr Thomas, although I am Mr Thomas. I am Mr bastard Thomas Lewis. Or is it Mr Lewis? Does anyone around here know who I am?" Michael was very drunk, confused, and loud. The stranger was a gentleman who knew Ben very well, therefore, he had escorted Michael home as best he could. He led Michael to the front door, trying to hold him upright. He then rang the doorbell and Gladys opened the door, looking at the state Michael was in. The gentleman says to Gladys, "Would you like me to take him upstairs for you, Mrs?" "My name is Gladys," she said. "Okay, Gladys, shall I?" "Only if you don't mind?" replied Gladys. This he did in a pattern of five steps upstairs, three steps back down the stairs. After a struggle, he dropped Michael on the bed and a very exhausted gentleman said to Gladys, "He's on the bed now. I've taken off his black tie and opened the top button of his shirt and I think he will sleep it off." Gladys offered him a cup of tea, but he needed to get home himself, so declined the offer and left the house. All was quiet throughout the rest of the night as Michael was too drunk to move, and he did, as they say, sleep it off. Early the next morning, Jane rang the house inquiring after Michael. Teresa answered and told her Nana Jane he was still in bed. Jane then asked, "Is Gladys there?" Teresa turned to Gladys, who was by the telephone, and asked if she would speak to Nana Jane. "Teresa," she said, "tell your Nana Jane I will speak to her, but not over the phone as what I wish to say to her, I will say to her face." Teresa, in shock, told Nana Jane what she had said. "Oh yes," said Jane. "I have plenty to say to her also. So please, Teresa, tell her we will talk soon. Unless she doesn't like the truth." Teresa passed the message onto her mother and purposely hung up the phone quickly. Gladys started shouting out loud, "Truth! Truth?! She doesn't know the meaning of the word. Wait till I see her. I'll give her a couple of home truths."

Gladys went upstairs to get dressed. Michael sat on the bed, and said to Gladys, "What on earth is the matter with you?" Gladys replied, "Ask your mother. Go on, ask your mother, because I'm telling you, Michael, you will be attending another funeral soon - hers." "That's right," Michael retorted, "make it about you when you know I'm suffering." "Yes, you're suffering, Michael; from a hangover," Gladys replied. Michael, in a childish voice, said, "Please, my love, don't hurt Jane. She's been through a lot in life." Gladys looked straight into Michael's eyes and said, "Get your priorities right, Michael. You should realise I have been through a lot marrying you with a mother like that. I'm not taking her shit anymore. But you, you can please yourself and go live with the dirty adulteress if you want. Then I'll be free of the two of you." Michael stood up in anger but fell back down on the bed. He shouted to Gladys, "Get out of my sight and out of my life, because you are a moll and no good, just like my mother says. Go on, get out!" he yelled. Gladys did just that; she grabbed her coat and left the house. All three siblings heard this but just kept quiet so as not to make matters worse.

Teresa made breakfast for everyone, only boiled eggs and toast, and called Terry and Tabitha to the kitchen table. All three were talking quietly at the table when they heard Michael moving around upstairs. He was muttering and laughing to himself, saying "Bloody women! All women are whores; all women are deceitful". Then they heard all of Gladys's shoes and clothes being thrown downstairs. He then opened an upstairs window and threw her handbags and makeup outside onto the lawn. Tabitha and Teresa ran outside and quickly picked them up. Terry took off in his car to see if he could find Gladys. He could not find her at Maisie's, so thought she might be at Nana Jane's, after the phone call earlier that morning. He got back in his car and drove up the hill to Nana Jane's house. He knocked on her door; Jane answered and said to Terry, "Come on in! How nice to see you, Terry. I haven't seen any of you to talk to due to the funeral and the passing of Uncle Ben." Terry looked at her angrily, and said, "Uncle Ben? Don't you mean Grandpa?" "Well, yes, I suppose so," replied Nana Jane. Terry then told her he was looking for his mother and asked "Has she been up here?" "No," replied Nana Jane. "But wait till she does." Terry said, "She's not happy with you either." Nana Jane replied, "If she comes here to upset me, I will call the police as I am an old lady." Terry had a quick look around then left. Whilst driving back, he spotted his mother on the other side of the road. She was heading to Nana Jane's house. He quickly turned the car around and asked Gladys to get in but she refused. Terry explained to her what Michael was doing at the house and that

Nana Jane was ready to call the police if she showed up. Gladys thought to herself that Jane could wait and got into Terry's car. Meanwhile, at the house, Michael was distraught, destroying pictures of him and Gladys's wedding day at the registry office. Teresa tried to stop him, but he only pushed her out of his way. There was glass everywhere. Tabitha was keeping out of his way, but trembling and shouting at her father to stop. Terry and Gladys tried to walk in through the front door, only to find shoes and clothes blocking the entrance, so they quickly went around to the back door. They opened the door only to hear Tabitha telling Michael, "Stop, please, Dad. Stop!" Michael saw Gladys and headed straight towards her, yelling, "Get out, you fucking bitch! Get out!" Gladys replied, "This is our home as well as yours, so *you* get out." Michael grabbed her by her hair, and Terry grabbed Michael. "Oh yes. Mummy's boy has come to the whore's rescue," said Michael, then he taunted Terry by saying "mummy's boy" over and over. Michael could still overpower Terry, which meant he managed to thump Gladys over and over before Terry, who was then helped by Teresa, got him to the ground. Teresa told Tabitha to phone the police, which she did, and they were at the house in minutes. The police stopped and held Michael, which meant Teresa and Terry could finally stop restraining their father. However, once again, they told Gladys they couldn't do anything as this was a domestic issue.

Gladys then phoned the hospital, telling them he was having another nervous breakdown and was being held by the police until the doctors came. Once again, Michael was telling the police what had upset him, and that it was not Gladys this time but his mother. "How would you feel if you were told a man was your father just after he died?" he asked them. He then started crying and appeared very weak and vulnerable. The doctors soon arrived, and Michael admitted to them that he hadn't taken his medication since before his father died as he'd had 'a lot to contend with', and this had obviously made matters worse, so they gave Michael an injection and took him back to hospital. The police left telling Tabitha, "You did the right thing calling us." Teresa put the kettle on, and she and Tabitha started picking up the clothes and shoes, whilst Gladys was picking up the glass. Maisie then called in to see Gladys, and they sat at the kitchen table with a cup of tea talking about the events of the day.

Gladys told Maisie, "I'm going to tell Jane just what she's doing to her son; wait until I see her." Gladys then told her, "The children have put up with this all their lives, but they are much older now and I am wondering what their futures will be like. I am hoping Teresa will marry soon; it's only right she does. She's been engaged for months now. Terry, however, hasn't got a girlfriend yet, so God knows about him. Tabitha will soon be leaving school. I think I'll try and get her a job where I work. She would like that." Maisie said, "What about Michael?" "Yes, what about Michael? I think I will divorce him. He should go and live with his mother," replied Gladys. Maisie, then looked at Gladys and said, "You must let your children make their own way in life; you cannot control their future. Surely Teresa will know when she wants to marry, never mind when she is expected to, and as for Tabitha, she too will find her own way. Terry is a young man, and boys are usually slower to grow up and mature than girls. Leave him to his own devices. Look what has happened to Michael. Secrets and lies catch up with people eventually, so surely, Gladys, happiness is more important than following old-fashioned morals and traditions, especially in Teresa's case?" Gladys explained that she wanted Teresa to marry as young girls could easily go off the rails, but Maisie disagreed with her. She then gave her a hug and left the house.

When Maisie left, Gladys phoned Myfanwy, telling her what had happened. She was so upset, saying that it was Jane's fault. The way Michael was behaving at the funeral, she wasn't at all surprised; as she said, he was very offensive to a lot of people. "So many things could have triggered the breakdown," said Gladys, and that was the question nobody could answer - was it a result of not taking his medication? Was it finding out Ben was his father? "We will never know, but most probably, it was the two combined that were to blame." Gladys talked for a while longer then said goodbye and hung up the telephone.

Weeks went by and Gladys carried on as usual, visiting Michael in hospital and worrying about her children, who, although grown up, weren't very happy. Gladys had her job to keep her busy, as did the children, and things weren't as tight as during previous hospital stays because the children gave more money and support. Gladys didn't know how long Michael would be in hospital this time; his recovery was slower than after previous breakdowns, which was a cause for concern for the doctors. His mother visited regularly, but she never saw Gladys, who kept out of her way to avoid upsetting Michael.

Chapter 2

Surprising Revelations

After months of treatment, Michael was now ready to be discharged, but before the doctors would discharge him, they called Gladys into a room for a chat. The room was all white and felt very claustrophobic and sterile. The doctors went on to say that Michael had told them that the reason he got ill was that she gave him an awful life, and had turned the children against him. Gladys could not contain her feelings anymore. This wasn't the first time he had told tales to the doctors, so she told them everything, even about his real father, which Michael had already told them himself during his admission to hospital. Then she added the fact that Jane had kept the secret until his father died. The doctors were shocked, as they were under the impression that only his mother really cared for him. They told her that they knew nothing of this. One doctor looked at Gladys and said, "We are so sorry. When people are having breakdowns, it usually occurs when they are under a lot of stress, and now, we see he was. He gave us a story of missing the love from his children as they had been brainwashed and lied to by yourself. But I must also tell you, his mother told us the same." Gladys was fuming, knowing Jane must have told Michael, during her regular visits, not to tell the doctors about Ben. She left the hospital with Michael, and Terry, who was waiting outside, took them home in his car. Knowing what he had done, Gladys couldn't look at Michael and never spoke a word during the journey home. Terry, looking at Gladys, realised something was wrong so he also kept quiet.

After settling Michael at home and giving him a cup of tea, Gladys asked Terry to stay with him as she needed to go out for a while. She had decided it was time to see Jane face to face, especially after the conversation with his doctors; her blood was boiling. She went to Jane's house and Jane opened the door. Gladys entered the hallway, and told Jane, "You stay away from the house and keep your lies to yourself. You're the slut, the adulteress, and the lowest form of human life ever." Jane was very shaken by this and said, "I'm going to phone the police if you don't leave". Gladys angrily said, "Oh, I am leaving, but I wish I had stabbed you all those years ago. You're hateful." Gladys left the house, slamming the door behind her. She felt so good that she was laughing out loud. She had finally got it all off her chest. "Whoopee!" she shouted, and went to Maisie's house to tell her everything. After Gladys's visit, Jane realised she couldn't visit Michael anymore as he was no longer in the hospital. This hurt Jane but it was her own doing, and she didn't know what to do. Her daughters were living away, and she knew she was going to die a very lonely woman. However, Gladys was still smiling and felt relieved, knowing there was no chance of his mother ever visiting and telling Michael to tell lies. The whole family hoped that Michael would take responsibility and take his medication, no matter what came his way, as this was the only way forward to a better life.

It was now early December; the weather had turned so cold, and it felt miserable outside. So, Gladys decided to put the decorations up, in the hope of forgetting the year they had just had. She said to Terry, "Let's cheer up the house and ourselves, shall we? Give me a hand with the Christmas tree, please, Terry?" Terry then helped Gladys set up the tree, and Tabitha helped her to decorate it. Meanwhile, Teresa was out with James doing the usual things - sitting in his father's house with Fred and Carol, James's sister, watching television. James had four sisters altogether, but Teresa never got to see them as they lived some distance away. He also has a brother in Australia named Lyndon. Suddenly, the door opened, and in came Linda, one of the sisters. She was very pretty with short blonde hair. Fred said, "Oh, what a lovely surprise! Do come in and meet Teresa, James's fiancée". Linda introduced herself to Teresa, and said, "I've heard so much about you, Teresa. Let's talk some more," and she sat beside her on the settee. Carol made teas and coffees and brought out a cake each for everyone. Fred asked Linda, "How come you're on your own? Is everything alright, my dear?" Linda replied, "No, Dad. Can I stay here with you for a while? I've left Gareth." "Of course, you can stay," replied Fred, "but what on earth happened?"

"He's been having an affair, Dad; I can't be with him right now." James, shocked, said to Linda, "You're welcome to the room that me and Teresa were going to decorate, as we still haven't got around to it. Would you like that?" "Thank you, James," she replied, "as long as you are both sure?" Teresa said, "Of course, Linda. We've never used it, so you're more than welcome." Suddenly, Teresa had a sinking feeling and felt quite unwell, so asked James to take her home. "Why do you want to go home now?" asked James. "Is it because of my sister and giving our room away?" Teresa replied, "No, not at all, James. I just don't know; I'm wondering if it's being in sad atmospheres all the time. I really need to find my happy place; I don't know if I can take all this uncertainty anymore. I just feel I need solid ground. But don't worry, I'll be ok; I always am."

James dropped Teresa off at home, and as she walked in, Gladys said, "You're early! You've hardly been out for two hours. Are you and James okay? Have you had a row?" "No, we haven't had a row," and she explained to Gladys about Linda. "How would that upset you?" asked Gladys. "I don't know, maybe it's all the misery surrounding me all the time. Why can't my life be like my friends? They are supported and loved by their families," Teresa told her. "Do you like the tree?" asked Tabitha. Teresa didn't even look at it. She said nothing and went to bed. Lying in bed awake, she was thinking, "Am I feeling sorry for myself? And I really don't know what love is. Is it like me and James, just good friends? I hear people talk about a spark. I don't know what that is. Maybe it's what I felt for David Kennedy; after all, I cried over him. I don't think I would cry over James if we finished, as I find life boring with him, but I know he loves me and he will always be by my side. But is this love one-sided? Oh, I don't know…" Finally, she drifted off to sleep.

The next day, Tabitha was going for an interview at the store where Gladys worked. She was very nervous, as this was the first piece of growing up she'd had to do. Teresa told her to come to the supermarket after to let her know how she got on. Later, a beaming Tabitha walked up to Teresa at the tills and said, "I got the job! I'm so happy, Teresa". She went on to tell her that she would be on the record counter and that she was to start the following Monday, two weeks before Christmas. "Congratulations, Tabitha!" Teresa replied, giving her a hug. "Now you can buy your own clothes and leave mine alone!"

That night, after Teresa finished work, she didn't want to go home, so she went to see her best friend, Elizabeth, just for a catch-up and a chat. She poured her emotions out to her and told Elizabeth that she couldn't make sense of her feelings. Elizabeth gave her a hug and they smoked a cigarette. Teresa was crying but she really didn't know why. Elizabeth continued to console her when her father walked in and said, "Oh dear, Teresa, I've never seen you like this. What on earth has brought this on?" Elizabeth explained to her father that she thought Teresa had just had enough of everything. "She needs some happiness," she went on to say. Her father left, saying, "We are all here for you, my love. You know that, don't you?" Teresa replied, "Yes. Thank you." Elizabeth told Teresa that her and James's relationship was nothing like hers and Bobby's, and they'd been together longer. "We go out to different places, and we laugh all the time. We go dancing, he buys me flowers most weeks, and I still get to see my friends. But you don't, Teresa. It's ages since we all saw you, isn't it?" She then went on to say, "Why don't you come out with us girls this Thursday? We're going dancing". Teresa replied, saying "I've still got to be in at eight-thirty, Elizabeth, and I know James wouldn't like it." Elizabeth replied, "He doesn't own you, Teresa, and you're eighteen now. They should have lifted the eight-thirty rule by now, especially if they know where you are and who you're with, shouldn't they?" Teresa replied, "I will try, Elizabeth. I'm sorry for crying on you. I will let you know; I will ask tonight." Teresa then said her goodbyes to Elizabeth and her parents and left for home.

Walking home, Teresa felt a lot better somehow and her mind was full of the nice feelings she should have been experiencing at her age instead of all the trauma and upset she'd been made to go through all her life. Teresa reached home and decided to ask her parents first, when they were both together, as that would be easier. She went upstairs as usual and got ready for when James arrived. When she came down, she said to both parents, "I have been invited by Elizabeth to start going out with the girls to the dance on Thursdays, so, I won't be in by eight-thirty." Gladys looked straight at Teresa and said, "What do you mean, eight-thirty? You're always half an hour late. And what would James think of that?" Teresa replied, "I'll tell him tonight that I can't see him on Thursdays." Gladys stood up and said, "If you think that's the proper actions of a girl who's engaged to be married, you've got another think coming. Do you want a reputation like Nana Jane? No, you don't, therefore, you're not staying out until God knows when," Gladys said angrily. Then Michael said to Gladys, "Stop talking about my mother like that. Teresa is nothing like her, and you must understand, she's eighteen now, not eight." He went on to say, "If she's old enough to marry, she's old enough to be going out to a dance." Teresa was in total disbelief; her father had stuck up for her. But Gladys stopped Teresa by saying, "While you're under my roof, you will abide by my rules. And that's the end of the conversation." Minutes later, James pulled up outside. So, Teresa went out to the car just so he wouldn't come into the house. Later that evening, she told James about the dance, and he was shocked that Teresa would want to go out with her friends instead of seeing him. "Don't you want to be with me anymore?" he asked. "Well, yes," Teresa said, "but I need more happiness, James. I need more, and I don't know what yet; something just isn't right." James was a stay-at-home man who never went drinking with friends, so he expected Teresa to follow suit. Then he said, "You do know what the problem is, don't you? It's your parents and the stupid time limit! Be fair, Teresa, we couldn't go dancing even if we wanted to." Teresa nodded to agree with him but deep down, she knew that if James asked Gladys, it would be, "Of course, James. You don't have to ask!"

They arrive at his father's house and Teresa sat down on the settee as usual, drinking tea and making small talk until it was time for her to go home, and as she left, Linda said to her, "Why have you got to be in so early?" Teresa replied, "I've just got to; it's like living in a prison," and she laughed as if it were a joke. Linda then turned to James and said, "Has she?" but James stopped her by saying, "Not tonight, Linda; it's a sore subject," and he fetched Teresa's coat and took her home.

Chapter 3

A Mystery Unravelled

James pulled up outside the house and they said their good nights. Teresa got out of the car, and for some reason, looked at her watch. It was nine-fifteen. Her mother was right - she was always late. As she opened the door, her mother shouted, "Well, what did James say about you going out without him?" "Nothing," Teresa replied, "but you are right, Mother, I am always late; a girl of eighteen coming in at this hour - how disgraceful is that, eh?" Gladys stood up and said, "No need to be sarcastic and rude, Teresa; it's for your own good." "Rules that make me unhappy?" Teresa went on to say. "Surely that isn't good for me, Mother? Oh, and James agrees." Gladys replied, "Well, if he does, then he must tell me to my face. I'm sure he wouldn't like his fiancée out all hours, would he now?" Teresa replied, "Well, I see Terry is still out; what can he possibly be up to? No good, I think". Gladys replied, "He's a boy. I've told you before; girls must keep up a good name, so just go to bed, Teresa. I've had enough arguing with you to last a lifetime." Teresa did just that. The following day, Teresa told Elizabeth that there was no way she could go out with the girls and explained all that happened. Elizabeth told her that she felt her life was being mapped out between her mother and James, and if it continued that way, she would live a very unhappy life. Teresa agreed but was so confused now that she didn't know how to alter the humdrum pattern of every day:

1. Get up in the morning.
2. Go to work.
3. Out with James.
4. Go to bed.

This was the pattern for five days, then on the weekend:

Saturday:
1. Have a lie-in.
2. Do the household chores for Mother.
3. Go out with James.
4. Go to bed.

Sunday:
1. Prepare Sunday lunch.
2. Eat Sunday lunch.
3. Out with James.
4. Go to bed.

And so on, and so on…. Boring! Boring! Boring!

The following day, Teresa was Christmas shopping and enjoying seeing the decorations in the stores, which did cheer her up a little, especially as Jean and Molly were with her; they were funny characters. "Let's all run away, and get somewhere to live with a very rich boy," Jean would say, and Molly would always add to her crazy ideas and say, "No boys, just men, no babies, plenty of money, and lots of fun." That's the picture of a good life, Teresa often thought to herself. After shopping, they would go to a café to talk, smoke cigarettes, and drink tea. The three girls had so much fun when they met up outside work. The sad reality was that Teresa couldn't join them every weekend as she always had her chores to do. Also, Jean and Molly worked some of the weekends since they worked on the shop floor. "Never mind," thought Teresa as she'd had a lovely day out today and felt great.

James was waiting at the house, busy talking to Gladys and drinking tea. As she opened the door, struggling with her bags, her mother started shouting, "What time do you call this, Teresa? James has been waiting almost two hours for you." Teresa replied, "Can't put a time on having fun with your friends, Mother". "That's enough!" said Gladys. Teresa chuckled as she took her Christmas shopping upstairs. "What have you bought, Teresa?" asked Tabitha. "Nosey, nosey, wait and see," Teresa said, then Tabitha went on to say, "I would have liked to have come with you shopping if you had

asked me, Teresa". "No, I went with my friends, Tabitha; you go with yours."
Since Teresa knew she would certainly report back to Mother as to what
went on, and what was said, this was a definite no. Gladys always thought
Jean and Molly were bad for Teresa, mainly because they were a little older
with different views on life. Teresa went back downstairs to put her coat
on and noticed Tabitha putting hers on too. Teresa asked, "Where are you
going?" "I'm coming with you. James said I could see Carol," Tabitha replied.
James just smiled as all three of them got into the car. When they arrived at
James's house, Carol and Tabitha went upstairs and were trying on clothes,
putting on makeup, and having a lot of fun which pleased Teresa. Linda
made everyone drinks and told Teresa that she and Gareth had made up
and were giving their marriage another chance. Teresa asked Linda, "What
about the other girl he was having an affair with?" Linda smiled and said,
"She dumped him, Teresa, as soon as she realised he was married. And he has
learned a hard lesson too; she didn't want him forever anyway. Now things
are going to change!" Teresa felt she would miss Linda when she returned to
her husband, as she was someone to talk to and like a big sister in the house.
Linda was leaving the next day, just in time for Christmas in her own home,
as she put it. Teresa quietly said to James, "When you take me home, you
must wait outside and give me time to wrap Linda's present. I will then give
it to you for you to take back home for her." This he did. Teresa lay awake in
bed that night, thinking, "Marriage isn't always a good thing. I really don't
know if I want to be married".

Christmas Day was here once again, and to Teresa's surprise, Tabitha had
given good presents to everyone. She really had grown up; still an annoying
teenager sister, but Teresa did care a lot for her. Terry, however, had given
his mother the task of getting his gifts. Teresa always gave her parents quite
expensive gifts, which always showed Terry's gifts up, and as usual, it did
the very same thing again this year. Whilst out in the kitchen, Terry called
Teresa into the hallway and said, "You must stop buying Mother expensive
presents after the way she treats you." "What are you saying? What do you
mean?" replied Teresa. "She's arguing with Dad behind your back; she just
wants you married off. And what the hell are you doing giving up all your
weekends off, cleaning, washing and cooking? I go where I want when I want.
She won't do it to me, so you need to stand up to her more, and Tabitha

agrees with me too." Gladys came out of the room and asked, "What are you two whispering about?" Terry just looked at Teresa and said, "You're the fool." Then he walked off into the room. Teresa went upstairs to talk to Tabitha and asked her what she and Terry had been talking about. Tabitha explained, "We feel sorry for you, Teresa. You know that day you went to Elizabeth's, and you didn't come straight home? Mother was saying you were out of control and Terry told her to lay off you and leave you alone. He was very worried, so both of us drove around looking for you." "I just needed to talk to Elizabeth that evening," Teresa said. "I didn't know what I was feeling; I was a little upset, that's all. I have lots on my mind right now."

After eating their Christmas dinner, they were all sitting around the fire watching television when James, Fred and Carol walked in bearing gifts. Everyone was happy and smiling, exchanging gifts with them. Carol and Tabitha decided to go out, as did Terry, so that meant the parents together with James and Teresa. Teresa knew what the subject would be – marriage. It wasn't long before Gladys said to Fred, "Fred, don't you think it's time for them to set a date for next year?" "Well," said Fred, "I'm sure they will let us know when they are ready". James joined in the conversation, saying, "Well, it's not going to be long". He then looked at Teresa and said, "Not long, is it, my love?" Teresa, embarrassed, replied to James, "When we're ready; who knows?" "That's right," said Gladys. "Teresa always answers a question with a question. Why can't you just say, Teresa?" "Because I don't know," she replied. Fred then asked Gladys if it would be a big wedding as he was prepared to contribute to the costs. "Oh, yes," said Gladys. "Church, the bells, and the choir; I want her to have the wedding I never had, Fred. After all, it's only once you can get married in church." Michael walked out of the room into the kitchen, as did Teresa, and left the others to their conversation. "Teresa, are you alright?" asked Michael. "Not really, Dad. I need to sort out what I want. I'm confused." Michael replied, "If you're not ready for marriage, Teresa, then you must not do it. You must be honest with yourself and James. Please, Teresa, go with your feelings, not with what is expected of you." Michael tapped her on her shoulder and went back into the room. Teresa then thought about what Tabitha had told her and her parents rowing behind her back now made sense. Her father was protecting her from her mother regarding the wedding. "Not once has she ever asked me if he is the one," she thought. "The truth is, James is the only boy I've ever dated. I have been with James for two years since I was sixteen, and are these unknown feelings I've been having premonitions? Mother really likes James and won't have a bad word said against him."

Teresa poured herself a drink and walked back into the room, when she heard Fred ask her mother if she had a lot of family. "No, Fred, I only have my stepbrother and his wife. Also, Maisie and Dan, and of course, Michael's family; they will make up the numbers." Fred went on to say, "Well, Gladys, we have a large family, so it should be around sixty to seventy people." Teresa thought, "They're planning my future; a future I'm not sure I want." She just glared directly at them. James noticed her reactions and whispered, "What's wrong? Isn't it nice our parents are getting along? What's the matter with you?" "I don't like them planning our future, James. Surely that should be for us to decide?" "But we want to be married, don't we?" he asked. "Of course, James, but when we are ready, not when they decide," she said. James turned to her and said, "They're only trying to help us, Teresa. Anyone would think you didn't want to marry me". Teresa bit her tongue as she nearly said, "I don't think I want to," but luckily, she didn't.

Michael then changed the subject completely by talking about gardening, as he knew Fred loved his garden, both flowers and vegetables.

An hour passed before Terry came back. Teresa told him what Michael had said to her, and how Mother had kept on about the bloody wedding. Terry sighed and said, "I told you so, Teresa. If you don't want to marry James, don't." "He's good to me, Terry, but I think we are more friends, or just used to each other," Teresa replied. "Well, I'm sorry, Teresa," said Terry, "but only you know what you feel. It's all in your hands, I'm sorry to say; nobody can choose for you." Terry then went to the kitchen, and Teresa, back to the lounge. Minutes later, Gladys and the girls laid out more food on the table for themselves and the guests to enjoy. No one mentioned the wedding again, which, of course, pleased Teresa. Later, after the Christmas film had finished, James, Fred and Carol stood up, thanking everyone for a wonderful day, and left the house. Gladys turned to everyone and said, "Help clear away, please, and help with the dishes?" To Teresa's surprise, everyone did.

So, Christmas Day was gone for another year, and Teresa was thinking about tomorrow, Boxing Day, as it was the only day of the year when she didn't see James. James liked following the fox hunting on Boxing Day and Teresa thought it was animal cruelty, so she never joined him. He went along with his farming friends and took his dogs. James's outlook on animals was completely different to Teresa's, and it was nothing for James to hold a rabbit and kill it. This she could never accept, nor did she want any part of it as her love for animals was unconditional; she preferred them to humans any day. On her way to bed that night, Tabitha asked her what she was doing the next day. Teresa replied, "I'm not sure yet. I feel a little at a loss, but also quite excited as I'm not sure what the day will bring. Why do you ask, Tabitha?" "Oh, I'm seeing Carol tomorrow. Fred is picking me up, and James asked me to invite you so that you'll be at the house when he gets home." Teresa was shocked that James wanted her to hang out with Tabitha and Carol at his father's house, so she said, "No. I won't be coming, Tabitha. I'm not sure what I'm doing". "Cheeky sod," she thought. "Does he want to keep tabs on me whilst he's out having fun? And on my only day of freedom?" Teresa then decided she wouldn't tell Tabitha what she was going to be doing, so she couldn't tell James, but she didn't really know herself yet.

The following morning came, and Teresa had a nice long lie in bed, then ran herself a bath. Tabitha had already left with Fred, and Terry was in his room playing music. It was a lovely place to think, in the bath, all nice and warm, cosy and quiet. It was there that Teresa decided not to worry herself about things that hadn't happened yet. "No more worrying about getting married, and live life for now, the present. I'm not going to think of the future anymore, well, not for now, anyway." She lay there lovely and calm, putting her toes up to the taps until it almost went cold. Out of the bath she got, wrapped herself in a towel, and headed to the bedroom. An hour later, she was dressed, hair done and makeup on, and ready to go out. As she came downstairs, she heard Gladys and Michael arguing in the lounge. Michael was asking Gladys to go with him to see Nana Jane as it was Christmas and he thought she shouldn't be on her own. "You go," Gladys said to him. "Go on if you want to, because I'm staying here." Then she suggested, "Why not ask Teresa to go with you? She's your favourite; the one you keep sticking up for. Go on, ask her. She might because she's just like her." Saying that she was like her Nana Jane hurt Teresa because she could never see any similarity to her Nana, but she soon realised it was just a way of Gladys hurting Michael. Not wanting to go with Michael, she grabbed her coat and boots, and quietly went out of the door.

Walking along the pavement, she soon found herself heading towards Elizabeth's house, so decided to knock on the door. Elizabeth answered and was so pleased to see Teresa. "Hello, hello," she said, hugging her tightly. "Come on in! How come you're here today? It's a lovely surprise," and she shouted to her parents, "Guess who's here?" Teresa always had a good reception when she visited Elizabeth's house. Later, Elizabeth and Teresa went out for a walk, visiting the other friends Teresa hadn't seen for a long time, and being Christmas time, most were home. Teresa was welcomed everywhere, by everybody and their parents. The drinks were flowing in every house, just like a pub crawl, but this was a friend's house crawl. Teresa and Elizabeth were laughing, and everyone was getting slowly drunk. They even wished the new year in even though it wasn't even here yet. Hours and hours went by, and Teresa and Elizabeth were holding each other up. They must have visited at least five houses, picking friends up along the way and toasting to everything. Happiness was an understatement; they loved each other. They were the best friends they could be. Elizabeth said, "Let's all make a toast!" The other girls were saying, "What? Another one?" "Yes," said Elizabeth, "a toast to friends, lifetime friends, girls whom no men can come between." Everyone raised their glasses and made a lifetime promise, which would most probably be forgotten by the morning. They partied all night until the early hours of the morning and didn't know who had called the taxi. One by one, they were dropped off at their homes. Teresa was last but one, so out she got saying goodbye to her other friend quite loudly, as you would expect, and walked up the path to her house. She put the key in the door and tried to creep in while removing her boots, but she then fell in the door. Teresa looked up, only to see an angry Gladys looking down at her. "You think this behaviour is funny do you, Teresa?" Laughing, Teresa said, "Merry Christmas, Mother!" Laughing quietly, Terry said to Gladys, "I'll help her upstairs". Gladys turned to him and said, "Yes, you do that, and I will deal with her in the morning. It's no good talking to her now." Terry took Teresa to her room, laughing all the way. "Come on, sis," he said, as he knew she didn't usually drink but was very pleased as she appeared to have had a good time. Teresa, still giggling, got herself undressed for bed, and Tabitha also started laughing and couldn't stop as she watched her sister. However, it wasn't long before Teresa fell fast asleep.

It was almost lunchtime the following day before Teresa got out of bed, with a banging head and feeling slightly dizzy. She looked in the mirror, with yesterday's makeup halfway down her face, and thought, "Oh, my God, I really look rough". She went to the bathroom to wash and clean her teeth. Gladys shouted up the stairs, "Teresa, James is here for you." "Great," thought Teresa. "I won't get a lecture or a row now James is here." Teresa quickly got herself dressed, put her makeup on and did her hair. On her way downstairs, she met Terry. He looked at her and smiled, saying, "Good night last night, was it, Teresa?" Teresa smiled back, saying, "Excellent, thank you." Gladys just looked angrily at Teresa, shaking her head but saying nothing. "Are you ready?" asked James. "Yes, I'm ready," replied Teresa, and they left the house and headed for the car. Only five minutes or less had passed before James asked Teresa what she had done yesterday. "I went out with Elizabeth," she said, "and we visited other friends." "You had a good time then, I hear?" said James. "What do you mean, you hear?" asked Teresa, feeling very uncomfortable with the remark, and the way he said it. "Oh, your mother told me you fell in the house severely intoxicated in the early hours of the morning. Is this true?" "If you mean did I have a drink and have fun with my friends, James, then the answer is yes." Teresa went on to say, "What about you? Did you kill any nice foxes yesterday?" "No, Teresa, you'll be glad to hear nothing was killed. Just tell me, Teresa, have I anything to worry about? You don't seem very happy lately." "James, you've nothing to worry about, it's just my bloody mother trying to run my life again. Surely you feel it too?" "Yes, they're all a bit full on, but my dad thinks you have big doubts about marrying me and about your future." Teresa replied, "Marriage is frightening me, James. They all seem to be full of arguments affairs, violence, and deceit and no happiness." James went on to say, "But you know I would never hurt you. Never raise a single finger to you. I love you, Teresa, and all I want is for us to be a married couple. You especially wouldn't be controlled or bogged down with chores." Teresa knew he was right and thought about what he said very seriously. "After all," she thought, "most of my friends are engaged, or have steady boyfriends. Maybe James and I could be happy? It isn't as if I don't care for him because I do. But if this is love, it's not all it's cracked up to be, is it?"

When they reached the house, Teresa walked into their room and noticed it was looking different. "Like it?" asked James. "Yes, it's beautiful," Teresa replied. He had put in all new skirting boards, lovely wallpaper and brilliant white paintwork. James had decorated it from top to bottom when Linda had left. "I decided to get it ready for when we move in together, when we're married, of course," he said. "Oh, my God," Teresa thought, "that bloody 'M' word again." Teresa was quite touched as he had done this as a surprise, and Fred then said, "He's been working through the nights, and finished it in the early hours this morning Teresa." Teresa then thought, "He was decorating as I fell in the house drunk; oh dear, how bad is that?" She turned around and headed for the kitchen, made drinks and walked into the lounge where Carol was sitting watching TV. Carol then asked her if she liked the room. "Yes," replied Teresa. "Can Tabitha and I be bridesmaids at your wedding, Teresa?" Carol asked, smiling. "Of course, you can, but it may be a bit of a wait, Carol." Carol then looked at Teresa saying, "No, it's going to be an Easter wedding, Teresa; that's only four months away." "No, it's not, Carol. Nothing has been arranged yet, and I, being the bride-to-be, should know." Carol, looking upset, left the room for a moment and walked back in with James. "That's another surprise, I hope, Teresa. Just before Christmas, I was talking to your mother whilst waiting for you to come home, and we thought it would be lovely to have an Easter wedding, but nothing is booked as you wouldn't enter the conversation or commit on Christmas day. Of course, if you don't want to…" The look on Teresa's face was plain to see. She was devastated; with tears in her eyes, she couldn't talk. Fred walked in, looked at Teresa and said, "You are a lovely caring girl, and I would be more than honoured to have you as my daughter-in-law, Teresa, but of course, you must set your own date. Nothing, I repeat, nothing is booked."

Of course, Fred was right, but everyone was thinking Easter, and Teresa felt the pressure was on her. She went to the bathroom and dried the tears from her eyes. She sat there for a while as she needed to be by herself. James hadn't mentioned the conversation between himself and her mother, and she felt betrayed as if between them they had been plotting, but at the same time, if she felt nothing for James, she shouldn't be leading him on. "How much longer can I put this off?" she wondered. James wouldn't understand if I said no, so what can I do? There is no way out, I must marry him, or finish with him, but I don't wish to lose him, or marry him!" She was more than confused. "Oh well," she thought as she left the bathroom, "it looks like I'm getting married." She went downstairs and said to James, "Easter is when we will marry." James was ecstatic. He was hugging Teresa and jumping up and down. Fred gave Teresa a big kiss on her cheek and opened a bottle of wine for a toast. Fred then said, "Raise your glasses to an Easter wedding for a very happy couple". Teresa could hardly drink hers as her stomach was still recovering from the night before. She felt different and couldn't understand what it was; she suddenly felt all grown up somehow. James then turned to Teresa and said, "I think we had better let your parents know that we have agreed on an Easter wedding, hadn't we?" "Yes," Teresa replied. So, with Carol in tow, they drove back to Teresa's house, where all the family were in the lounge, watching television. James then announced to Gladys and Michael, "We are to be married at Easter, just like everybody wanted." Gladys was beaming but you could tell that Michael was holding back his real emotions. Terry, however, whispered, "I hope for your sake, sis, you've made the right decision." "I think I have, Terry," she replied. "He would never hurt me; I am quite sure of that. And I won't have to put up with the life here now, will I?" Then she thought, "Why did I say that? Is that the reason I agreed? Oh well," she thought to herself, "it's done now."

Surprisingly, Gladys never did mention the drunk Boxing Day night. She was different; she was kind to Teresa, treating her like she was all grown up now, and no longer a child. But of course, she got her wish. Michael, however, continued to be very moody when the wedding was mentioned. Gladys blamed the cost as Michael had to borrow from the bank. "Let's cut the cost down," Teresa went on to say. "I don't need the choir, or the bells or the very expensive hotel for the reception." Gladys stuck to her guns and wouldn't compromise and told Michael that his mother would be invited if he wanted her there. The time seemed to fly by with dress fittings, suit fittings, attending the church to hear the banns being called, appointments with the vicar, and of course, the photographer, flowers and cars. Teresa would go to work for a rest, but still found the conversation in work revolved around wedding talk. Jean and Molly, of course, were invited, as was Elizabeth, her best friend. She was to be the maid of honour.

One afternoon, whilst at work, Teresa's boss asked to see her. Teresa thought, "I don't want the sack now. I'm getting married, I need the money." She slowly entered the office when her boss asked her. "Have you anywhere to live, Teresa, when you marry?" "Not really," she replied. "Just a room at James's house; I will be living with his family." He then told her that the flat above the store was soon to be vacant if she would like to rent it. Teresa jumped at the chance and thanked her boss. "The rent will be four pounds a week, Teresa, taken out of your wages. Is that alright?" It was more than alright; it meant she wouldn't have the thirty-minute journey each day to work. Teresa was beaming. Everything appeared to be going more than well, and she told James that evening. He was more than happy, and they were going to view the flat the following day after work. When she told Gladys about the flat, she was pleased and asked Teresa if she could go with them to see it. Teresa said yes, so, after work the next day, all three went to view the flat, which was huge. The lounge was massive – so big you could hold a dance in it. It had two large bedrooms, a bathroom and a kitchen. Everything was falling into place, and it was very exciting. Teresa felt independent, her own self, more mature; all sorts of lovely feelings suddenly came her way. Weeks went by too fast really, and the cake still hadn't been made yet, as a friend of Gladys's from work was making it but suddenly became ill. So, Teresa then asked the local bakery to do it for her as this had to now be rushed in time for the big day.

Tabitha was home one evening on her own with Gladys and Michael when suddenly, they started rowing. It was about the guest list. Gladys felt that she should invite more of her friends, as there were a lot on Michael's side and also on Fred's. Michael said, "This is costing enough as it is without feeding the whole town." Gladys, fighting back, said, "We're inviting your mother, aren't we? Even after she made you a bastard." "Throw that up again, Gladys, and I will reveal your past," he was saying. Tabitha was curious and asked, "What's your past, Mother?" Gladys looked at Michael and said, "Thank you very much for that, Michael. Everything is destroyed between us now; you promised me that would never be spoken of again." Michael angrily replied, "I'm fed up with the kids being made to believe that you are whiter than white, and pushing Teresa into a marriage based on morals." This infuriated Gladys, so she fought back saying, "Families should have standards, and as none of mine or yours did, all I ever wanted was to bring the kids up right, and behave how they should in society," replied Gladys. She then looked at Tabitha, got up and slammed the door on her way out. Michael sat down and looked at the puzzled expression on Tabitha's face. "Be a good girl, Tabitha, and put the kettle on," he said. With that, Teresa walked in and immediately sensed an atmosphere. It wasn't good. She went into the kitchen and asked Tabitha what was wrong. Tabitha filled her in on the row, stating that Mother had a secret past. Teresa went upstairs and found her mother crying. She sat alongside her on the bed, and said, "What's wrong now? What did he mean about your past?" "I've had it with him now, Teresa. Years of arguing and torment and he can't even keep a secret I told him years ago. With all his health issues, he never did pull this card out of the pack, and that I admired him for, but now that's it with him," she said. Teresa asked, "What could be so bad as to make you cry and feel like this?" "Alright, Teresa, I will tell you as I know this is never going away." Gladys then went on to explain.

Her mother had lived in London and fell in love with an American soldier. She fell pregnant and had Gladys. Then she found out that the soldier was married. All this was during the war, and he was soon to be going back to America. This was a very bad thing in those days as she knew she would bring shame on the family and it would ruin her mother's life. Her actions were scandalous, and because of all this, her mother, Gladys's grandmother, decided she would bring up the baby as her own. So, Gladys's mum was now to be recognised as her sister. Growing up, Gladys thought her mum was her mum and was not told any different until her mother fell ill and could no longer look after her. They started bombing the hell out of London, so her sister, (her mother) sent her to Wales as one of the evacuees for her own safety, along with thousands of other children of all ages. Teresa then asked, "How did you find out? How old were you?" "I must have been around fourteen or fifteen," she replied. She then went on to say, "I had a case full of clothes, and I, like everyone else, was very scared and crying. I did not want to go. My sister took me to the train station. I remember it was very smoky, and you could hardly see who was who. I was looking for my friend, then realised she was standing right beside me. My sister then looked straight into my eyes and said, "Gladys, I am not your sister, I am your mother. Mum was your grandmother. You needed to know the truth." There were tears running down her cheeks as she went on to say, "Listen, please listen, Gladys; in your case is a letter I have written with a full explanation of the truth." The station men were telling people to get all the children onto the train now, as it had to leave the station. I felt I was pushed onto the train. I tried to see out of the window but could not, and that was the last time I saw her. And that, Teresa, is that." "Surely, though," said Teresa, "there was nothing you could do about that, so why the secrecy?" Gladys replied, "Don't you see, Teresa? I am also a bastard. Born out of wedlock to an English mother and an American father who, incidentally, was married and wanted nothing to do with my mother. That is why morals are important; if women crossed the line, they would get themselves a bad name. But on the other hand, men can do as they like with no repercussions." Teresa asked her, "Do you know your father's name?" "No," Gladys went on to say, "as the only thing the letter told me was that he was a married American soldier. A lot of people were killed in the war, and I think if my mother were still alive, surely, she would have come to Wales for me. Or maybe not if she had a fresh start. She could have got married and had a family, and if so, how would she explain me? I am her dirty secret, best forgotten," Gladys said. Teresa thought long and hard about this and realised that how you behave today can affect you tomorrow. The cover-ups, the secrets, the forbidden love affairs, ghosts in your closet, as they say. Teresa even thought back to the accusation, referring to Gladys and Robert having an affair, and wondered if her mother was also hiding another dirty secret. "Does Nana Jane know about this?" asked Teresa. "Oh yes," replied Gladys, "that is where her terminology comes from – "You're not good enough for Michael, trollop, whore. Just like your mother." You see, Teresa, you get judged by what your relations before you did, and so on. Good stock, bad stock, that is what they call it." "Well," Teresa said, "that is the past. You can't change it, but you can change your future. So how about a cup of tea? Tea is the answer for everything, isn't it?" Teresa asked. "Yes, you're right," said Gladys. "Let's go downstairs."

As she opened the bedroom door, Teresa saw Tabitha listening at the top of the stairs. "Did you hear all that?" asked Teresa. "Yes," replied Tabitha. "Oh, well," said Teresa, "it saves me explaining anything to you later. Please tell Terry, will you?" she said, smiling away as she walked downstairs. Sat in the chair was a very worried, unhappy Michael. He stood up as Gladys walked into the room. She turned her head and said, "I've told the kids where I come from now, so I've passed the unknown of my roots onto them." Michael replied, "Don't be so silly; this news makes no difference to them." All Gladys would say was, "Time will tell."

Weeks went on with a divide between Gladys and Michael, however, they never had a cross word, but it felt as if a storm was brewing, or a volcano waiting to erupt. Luckily, all efforts and thoughts were now to do with the wedding, as time was approaching quickly, and James was busy planning the honeymoon. They both booked their time off work and had suitcases packed. They packed a variety of clothes as British weather can never be taken for granted, and it was April. With the help of Michael, they decorated their flat and had a cooker installed, then they furnished it as best they could with what little money they had. Michael kept visiting his mother, but still, she was not allowed into the house. Michael never mentioned her name as Gladys would become extremely angry, yet she always wondered what was being said. However, as long as she was not causing rows, Gladys was fine.

Chapter 4

Temperance

The wedding was only a week away, and Teresa wanted to visit her doctor to discuss taking the birth control pill. She felt she was her own person, even though she was still a very young eighteen. She did get her birth control pill and kept it to herself, not telling anyone. She didn't want children right now; it was too soon, and there were too many insecurities. And now she felt she had full control.

The next few days were manic with final dress fittings, making sure all the preparations were in place, and then, before she knew it, the big day was here; the Easter wedding. Teresa, Tabitha and her mother went to the hairdressers, as did the maid of honour and the other bridesmaids. They all got themselves dressed at Gladys and Michael's house. They all looked so beautiful. Terry walked into the room in his suit, looking amazing, as did Michael. Flowers arrived - bouquets for the bride, bridesmaids, and maid of honour, and buttonhole carnations for the men. Teresa was nervous and started to shake. She was approached by Gladys, who held her hands and said, "This is completely normal, so don't worry. You look so beautiful, Teresa, and I feel proud of the young woman you have become." The big black wedding cars arrived to take them to the church. Teresa smiled as she noticed they had put big white ribbons across the fronts of them, and actual chauffeurs stood outside, ready to open the car doors. Teresa was feeling like a real-life princess. Everyone except Teresa and her father had now left for the church. Teresa noticed her father crying. "I'm sorry, Teresa, I just can't help it," he said. He was shaking. He couldn't control his hands, so Teresa held his hands as her mother had held hers. "When I'm looking at you, Teresa, I wonder, how did I make such a beautiful daughter? Please tell me, you weren't made to feel that you had to get married, Teresa, because you know you don't have to. We can stop this now. You only have to say you don't want to marry." Teresa, forgetting her nerves, looked into his eyes and said, "Father, when have I ever done what I was told?" Michael burst out laughing and said, "You know, Teresa, you're right, you never have. You have the strongest character out of the three of you!" "Well, there we are then; are we ready?" she asked. She held her father's arm and they stepped outside. Michael was smiling as he walked out with his daughter on his arm. The neighbours had all come out to see her, and the photographer was clicking away. At that moment, Teresa looked up at the skies above her. The clouds were gathering, and she thought, "Clouds, please don't rain on my parade." Standing by the car, the chauffeur opened the door for them. The car was driven very slowly, and people were turning around to see if they could see the bride. They reached the church, and the bridesmaids were waiting. Elizabeth walked towards the car door to help Teresa out in her dress. She remembered the beaming smile on her father's face. This was the happiest she had ever seen him in her life and knew this image of her father was one she would never forget because, at that moment, she felt a warmth, a love, a connection with her father that she had never felt before. She could not understand this feeling but enjoyed every second.

'Here Comes the Bride' was playing on the organ when Michael said to Teresa, "This is it, my love. Shall we walk?" "Yes," replied Teresa. The bridesmaids held the long train of her dress up from the floor, and with her veil over her face, and her beautiful white dress just flowing, an extremely nervous Teresa and a very proud and happy Michael proceeded to walk down the aisle. The bells rang out, and the choir sang. The ceremony was underway. James and Teresa exchanged vows and wedding rings, then went out to the back of the church to sign the register. They were now man and wife. Again, the bells were ringing, as James and Teresa walked back down the aisle to the front of the church, and outside for photographs. Confetti was thrown, and passers-by stopped once again to see the bride. Then she and James both got into the chauffeur-driven car which would take them to the hotel. There, they were greeted on arrival by the hotel owners, ready for the reception. James and Teresa stood at the entrance to greet their guests, all congratulating them on their big day. Nana Jane pretended to lose her balance and grabbed Teresa's dress, almost tearing it. She did say "sorry", but Teresa felt it was deliberate. Myfanwy and Winnie, wearing big, beautiful hats, were more than dressed up. They looked amazing. The three-course meal was served, and James and Teresa cut the cake. After that, Teresa felt relaxed and happy. She looked at her father, who was chatting and still wearing that massive, proud smile she had seen earlier. She looked for her mother but could not see her, but minutes later, saw her return with Uncle Robert. They really looked suspicious and she hoped no one else had seen it, as this could spoil her big day. It was not long before Terry and Tabitha were whispering, so Teresa gave them a puzzled look. What did it mean? Terry came over and said to Teresa, "See, Teresa, I've been right all along. I caught them kissing and hugging, holding hands out in the foyer. But don't say anything to anyone," he said. That was the last thing Teresa would do as she didn't want to upset her father.

Time went on and soon it was time for Teresa to go home to get changed, and then return to the hotel. It was only an hour before the car came to take them to the train station. James and Teresa were going to Blackpool for their honeymoon, a place Teresa had not been, but saying that, she hadn't been anywhere apart from the beach holiday she'd had years ago with her family and the stay with Uncle Robert. "This was normal anyway," she thought, as none of her friends were well-travelled. The car came back to the hotel to escort James and Teresa to the train station. To their surprise, a lot of the guests followed in their cars to see the happy couple off. They threw more confetti over James and Teresa, and on the train, as they boarded, even a bin was put on by one of the guests. The train started to pull away, and someone Teresa didn't know shouted, "Have a good time, Mr and Mrs Williams." Teresa's happiness for that day suddenly stopped. She didn't like her new title but wondered why. James turned to her and said, "Let's take a seat, Teresa, It's quite a long journey." This she did and thought to herself, "Have I made a massive mistake?" She was then trying to hide her feelings from James, and forcing smiles as and when he looked at her. Teresa knew at that precise moment, that she might have made the biggest mistake of her life. Feeling extremely uncomfortable, Teresa knew she had to continue to appear as happy as she could be, for James's sake, and everyone else's.

They arrived in Blackpool with cases in hand and took a taxi to the pre-booked B&B. Being April, the weather was not that good, but they still enjoyed their stay, as they walked along the promenade and ate chips. They also visited a few places of interest in Blackpool such as the famous Tower Ballroom and a theatre, and James bought Teresa a black and white teddy bear as a remembrance of their honeymoon in Blackpool. A week was not very long, and it soon became time for the return home, but both had another week off work to enjoy their new home in town. They boarded the train, knowing Terry would be waiting at the station at the other end to take them home. It didn't seem to take that long before they arrived back in their hometown, and, as they got off the train, they could see Terry waving. "How was Blackpool?" Terry asked, "Good. How was it at home?" Teresa asked. "Frosty," he replied. When Teresa asked why, Terry explained, "Michael practically lives in the back room now, because Gladys wants nothing to do with him." "Well," Teresa said, "they appeared good at the wedding. What's gone wrong?" "She won't forgive him regarding her past, Teresa, but both you and I know what's behind it, don't we?" Teresa thought what she always thought, "Here we go again," but this time she did not have to live in the atmosphere. This made her smile again.

On arrival at the flat, she saw all the wedding presents laid out in the middle of the room, and in one corner was a glass cabinet, a wedding present from her parents. She was so happy, and she and James opened the presents one by one, whilst reading the well-wishing cards. They both felt extremely happy, and they still had to decide what they would buy with the envelope of money that Fred and his family had given them. Teresa also knew she had to visit home in the next few days but didn't want anything to burst the bubble she was in, so she left it for a bit longer. The week was coming to an end, so James and Teresa jumped in the car to visit Michael and Gladys. As soon as they walked in, both parents came to greet them. The kettle went on and everyone seemed happy. The talk was about the honeymoon and the presents. Tabitha was home, so, Teresa asked, "Aren't you supposed to be at work today, Tabitha?" "No," she replied. I got the sack. I'm going to start in the sweet shop next week." "Why did they sack you?" asked Teresa. "Giving the wrong change, Teresa. It's all this new money," she went on to say. "Well, how will you manage in the sweet shop?" Teresa asked. "Because I've been practising, and I'm hoping you will help me. Will you?" "Of course, I will!

You will have to show me how far you have got and we will go from there. Is that okay?" she asked. "More than okay," Tabitha replied. Teresa went to the kitchen to make another cup of tea and glanced into the back room. There, she saw most of her father's belongings, including his pipe and slippers. "Terry was right yet again," she thought. On her return to the room, Gladys asked Teresa and James, "When are you thinking of starting a family?" But to Teresa's surprise, James answered very quickly, saying, "Oh, not yet, Gladys, it will be a while, I think." James and Teresa had never discussed the subject of children, and James didn't know she was on the pill, and neither did her mother. No one knew - it was Teresa's little secret. "Anyway, why should they know? It's nobody else's business," she thought to herself.

Over the following weeks, Teresa and James were back at work, and in the evenings, Teresa was helping Tabitha with the new decimalisation, or new money, as she called it. Tabitha found it hard going from pounds, shillings and pence to pounds and pence. But finally, later, she grasped it, just in time to serve in the shop instead of stacking the shelves. Life was much easier for Teresa. No tensions in her new home, nobody telling her where to go, or who to see, and no time limits on her life. She was, you might say, finally, her own woman. She got to see her friends a lot, and both Molly and Jean took their dinner breaks in her flat above the store. Elizabeth and her boyfriend Bobby, who were themselves soon to be married, were regular visitors.

Was the marriage to James the right decision? Will Teresa have her happy ever after? Will she have a rose garden? Or have children? No matter what, she is now in control of her life. She makes her own decisions, good or bad. Only time will tell. Everything in moderation won't hurt, she says, as she now has the power to pull back, go forward, and try to build herself a happy future, and maybe not look back on her childhood. One promise she has made to herself is that when she has her own children, no way will they be brought up in fear, violence, and insecurity. Instead, she will do her utmost to give them the happiest childhood she can, and as much love and consideration as she can possibly give. She feels very deeply that this is a very good base for adulthood, and any unplanned surprises they may endure throughout their life. They will be more than capable to cope with anything, and hopefully, they will be independent and strong. Most importantly, though, she will make sure that the path they choose in life will be of their own choosing.

Only sensible boundaries will ever be in place. The question lies within. How will life treat Teresa? Will her siblings cope? Will the parents stay together? One thing is for sure, Teresa will definitely take charge of her life, and if you're interested, she will come back to let you know. Time will tell, as her mother says.

THE END.

Morals or immoral?
Who are we to say?
Who makes up the boundaries
Of betrayal felt each day?
The rules of rightful conduct,
Ethicality and the truth.
Legalities and principles
Embedded in our youth.
Must we all conform to this;
Express ourselves by law,
Convincing our own character
Of the limits we endure?
Such actions, they can crush us.
They will eat into our soul.
Secrets, lies, unhappiness
Are out of our control.

B.A. JONES.

Lightning Source UK Ltd.
Milton Keynes UK
UKHW020259080223
416610UK00016B/2030